Hunger for her was pushing him over the edge.

If he kissed her—Hell. What was he thinking? He was supposed to be watching over her.

He walked out onto the porch, seeking distance, but Meghan followed. "You know you really are a cowboy at heart," she said. "Seeing you on the ranch, I get it."

"I'm not that complicated once you get to know me."

"How well did I know you when we were dating?"

He turned to her. "I couldn't say. We didn't do a lot of talking. We were too consumed with the physical side of the relationship." Somehow he'd let the conversation take a bad turn. "Are you sure you want to get into this?"

"What I want is for you to kiss me, Durk. The way you did when we first met."

"I don't think that's a good idea."

"Then stop thinking."

JOANNA WAYNE

BIG SHOT

HARLEQUIN®

entertain, enrich, inspire™

To my sisters, Mary, Barbara, Linda and Brenda. Always great to get together. You warm my heart. And to everyone who's ever loved a real or fictional cowboy! And thanks to my editor, who makes me want to keep writing Harlequin Intrigue novels even after fifty-plus books.

ISBN-13: 978-0-373-74704-7

BIG SHOT

Copyright © 2012 by Jo Ann Vest

Recycling programs
for this product may
not exist in your area.

www.Harlequin.com

Printed in U.S.A.

ABOUT THE AUTHOR

Joanna Wayne was born and raised in Shreveport, Louisiana, and received her undergraduate and graduate degrees from LSU-Shreveport. She moved to New Orleans in 1984, and it was there that she attended her first writing class and joined her first professional writing organization. Her debut novel, *Deep in the Bayou*, was published in 1994.

Now, dozens of published books later, Joanna has made a name for herself as being on the cutting edge of romantic suspense in both series and single-title novels. She has been on the Waldenbooks bestseller list for romance and has won many industry awards. She is also a popular speaker at writing organizations and local community functions and has taught creative writing at the University of New Orleans Metropolitan College.

Joanna currently resides in a small community forty miles north of Houston, Texas, with her husband. Though she still has many family and emotional ties to Louisiana, she loves living in the Lone Star State. You may write Joanna at P.O. Box 852, Montgomery, Texas 77356.

Books by Joanna Wayne

HARLEQUIN INTRIGUE
1001—24 KARAT AMMUNITION*
1019—TEXAS GUN SMOKE*
1041—POINT BLANK PROTECTOR*
1065—LOADED*
1096—MIRACLE AT COLTS RUN CROSS*
1123—COWBOY COMMANDO‡
1152—COWBOY TO THE CORE‡
1167—BRAVO, TANGO, COWBOY‡
1195—COWBOY DELIRIUM
1228—COWBOY SWAGGER†
1249—GENUINE COWBOY†
1264—AK-COWBOY†
1289—COWBOY FEVER†
1308—STRANGER, SEDUCER, PROTECTOR
1325—COWBOY CONSPIRACY†
1341—SON OF A GUN**
1361—LIVE AMMO**
1383—BIG SHOT**

*Four Brothers of Colts Run Cross
‡Special Ops Texas
†Sons of Troy Ledger
**Big "D" Dads

CAST OF CHARACTERS

Meghan Sinclair—A private investigator who precariously walks the thin line between daring and duty.

Durk Lambert—CEO of Lambert, Inc. He's still a cowboy at heart and lives by the Cowboy Creed.

Bill Evers—Meghan's bodybuilder neighbor, who rescues her when she's attacked in her condo.

Lucy Delmar—Meghan's sister.

Ben Conroe—Meghan's assistant, who is murdered in their office.

Detective Sam Smart—He's in charge of investigating Ben Conroe's murder.

Dr. Levy—Meghan's doctor after she's attacked.

Connie Latimer—She's hired Meghan to find her sister's killer when the cops didn't.

Roxanne—Connie's murdered sister.

Edward Byers—A possible suspect in Ben's murder.

Carolina Lambert—Durk's mother.

Damien and Tague Lambert—Durk's brothers.

Belle—The foster daughter of Emma and Damien.

Alexis Lambert—Tague's wife.

Tommy Lambert—Alexis and Tague's son.

Sybil—Durk's aunt.

Pearl—Durk's grandmother.

Chapter One

Meghan Sinclair smiled as she exited the elevator to her fifth-floor condominium in downtown Dallas. Her afternoon coffee date had been a resounding success.

Her condo was at the end of the empty hallway, near the stairwell. Meghan slipped out of her shoes about halfway to her door and let her aching tootsies sink into the deep carpet. She slowed enough to bend over and hook the leather shoe straps with a crooked finger.

It was nice to live in luxury, thanks to the generosity of a former client who owned the complex. The fancy handbag was a bit of overkill for this time of day, but it and her dress had done their job. He'd given her a heck of a deal after she'd been instrumental in finding his daughter's killer. The depraved maniac had been arrested and tried and was now serving a life sentence. Case closed.

If she ever married and had a family, the condo would be too small. But if her love life kept to the same trajectory it was on now, that might never happen.

The door to the stairwell opened as she retrieved her key fob from the silver clutch. She fit her key into the lock before looking up, certain it was Mr. Muscles who lived two doors down.

A bodybuilding fanatic, Bill Mackey claimed elevators were for wimps. But then again, Mr. Muscles didn't own one pair of stilettos.

Meghan spun around at the sound of heavy breathing and running footsteps. A man bound into the hallway, masked and dressed in black. Definitely not her neighbor. She pushed through her door and tried to slam it shut behind her.

His foot stopped it. Two strong gloved hands closed around her neck, pressing so hard they blocked her airway.

Her P.I. self-defense skills were ingrained and automatic. She jerked upward, bucking hard with her head while she reached into her purse for her pistol. One of the attacker's hands left her throat, but before she could aim, her body started jerking uncontrollably.

She spotted his stun gun as her pistol fell from her shaking fingers. The attacker kicked her weapon in front of them as he pushed her flailing body into the condo, knocking her to the floor. When she tried to stand, he shoved her and sent her slamming into the wall.

The room began to spin. The scone and coffee she'd just eaten came up, mixed with blood. The last thing she saw was his body coming at her like a demolition ball bent on destruction.

The last thing she heard was her own terrified scream for help.

DURK LAMBERT STEPPED out of Lambert Towers and was greeted by blinding sunshine and a brisk breeze. The perfect fall afternoon, low seventies and not a cloud in sight. Just the kind of weather he needed to kick off his much-needed vacation.

His black Jaguar was waiting for him in front of the towering skyscraper, motor running with Miguel behind the wheel. Durk shed the jacket of his suit coat as Miguel climbed out of the car.

"Good afternoon, Mr. Lambert. Great weather to start a vacation."

"Couldn't ask for better," Durk agreed.

"Are you leaving town?"

"I'm leaving the city but going no farther than the Bent Pine Ranch." He loosened the knot in his tie, yanked it from around his neck and tossed it in the backseat with his jacket. "Good-bye, ties. Hello, boots and jeans."

"Good for you, boss man. Have a nice Thanksgiving."

"Thanks, Miguel. You, too. Do you have plans?"

"I'm driving down to Brownsville to spend a couple of weeks with my daughter and her family. Plan to do some fishing and roast one of their farm-raised goats over a spit. Now that's eating."

"Nothing like good *cabrito*," Durk agreed. He shook Miguel's wrinkled hand and climbed behind the wheel. He waited until Miguel had rounded the car and was back on the sidewalk before pulling into traffic.

The man was thin and slightly stooped, his weathered face showing the strain of seventy-seven years of living. He'd been a fixture around Lambert Inc. as long as Durk could remember.

He'd retired as maintenance engineer eight years ago when a heart condition had forced him to slow down. He'd come back on the payroll five years ago when his wife died.

He claimed he hated the empty house after so many years of marriage and he liked to keep busy. As long as he wanted to hang out at Lambert Inc., Durk would make certain they found a few non-stressful things for him to do.

The afternoon traffic was heavier than usual.

It was still one full week before Thanksgiving, but already the stores were decorated and pandering for holiday shoppers to give into their whims and the store's enticements.

Shopping was the furthest thing from Durk's mind. After the summer and autumn he'd had, he needed to get back in the saddle again. And to reacquaint himself with his family.

While he'd been traveling back and forth to the Middle East working on a new project that was a go and a merger that wasn't, his brother Tague had taken the plunge into wedlock and instant fatherhood.

No one had been more shocked at that than Durk—unless it was Tague himself. But Tague had adjusted well and had never seemed happier. Neither had his brother Damien, who'd been married for four months now.

Marriage and family weren't in Durk's foreseeable future—if ever. Some men were cut out for family life. Some weren't. He fell into the latter category.

Besides, the one time he'd let himself fall hard for a woman, it had ended badly. Talk about messing with his mind. No way would he go there again.

He turned at the light and headed toward I-45. He was almost to the freeway when his cell phone rang. He punched on his hands-free receiver.

"Durk Lambert."

"Glad I caught you, Durk. Are you still in Dallas?"

He tensed at the apprehension in his mother's voice. "I just left the office. What's up?"

"Sybil's friend Bessie George called. She said Sybil started having chest pains while they were out shopping. She called an ambulance and they took Sybil to Grantland Hospital."

"How long ago was that?"

"I just got the call. Bessie was on her way to the hospital to be with Sybil, but she's stuck behind a fender bender and traffic's at a standstill."

"That's Dallas for you. Traffic's moving here. I'll stop by the hospital now and check on Sybil."

"Thanks, son. Call me on my cell phone as soon as you see her. I'm driving in as well, but it will take me over an hour to get there from the ranch this time of day."

"Just hang tight until I call you back, Mom. No use for you to make the trip unless they're going to admit her. The last two times that Aunt Sybil rushed to the emergency room, it turned out to be acute indigestion."

"Yes, but you never know, Durk."

"I'll know after I talk to the doctor. Pour yourself a cup of coffee and try to relax. I'll get back to you as soon as I find out something."

"I guess that does make more sense than rushing into the city before I know if it's serious."

"Perfect sense," he agreed.

Durk's hands tightened on the wheel, the tension returning to his muscles. In spite of his reassurances, he was concerned about his aunt. She was his father's older sister—not that she was old. Her sixty-fourth birthday was coming up in a matter of weeks. She had lived with them for years, ever since her husband had died from a massive heart attack at the young age of fifty-eight.

The rambling old ranch house that had been in the Lambert family for generations served them all well. Aunt Sybil and his grandmother each had a private suite on the first floor. His mother was still in the master suite that she'd shared with his father before his untimely death, though she'd offered it to Damien and Emma when they'd married. They'd decided the west wing was the better choice for them, probably because it offered more play space for their foster daughter, Belle. Tague and his new wife, Alexis, and stepson, Tommy, had the suite on the second floor above Damien's, though they were already planning to build their own cottage on the ranch.

Durk's quarters were just off the huge billiards and game room on the second floor in the east wing of the house. He didn't need much space since when he wasn't traveling he spent most of his time in his penthouse condo in downtown Dallas.

In less than twenty minutes, he was standing at the admittance desk in the E.R. The young blonde nurse on duty looked a bit harried, but she managed a smile when she looked up at him. "How can I help you?"

"My aunt, Sybil Ratcliff, should have arrived by ambulance in the last few minutes. I'd like to check on her."

"Yes. I think the doctor is with her now." The nurse rifled through a half-dozen admittance slips. "She's in Room Four. I'll have someone escort you back there. You say she's your aunt?"

"Yes, I'm Durk Lambert."

"Durk Lambert." She repeated the name as she placed her hands on the counter, showing off her perfectly manicured nails and her ringless wedding band finger. This time her smile lit up her face. "Actually, I'll walk you to your aunt's room. If there's anything I can do to help, don't hesitate to let me know. My name's Pam."

She looked around and motioned to a middle-aged nurse who was adding information to a chart. "Can you man the desk for a minute, Ethel? I need to see that *Durk Lambert* finds his aunt."

Ethel eyeballed Durk, nodded and smiled conspiratorially. "Sure. Take your time."

He felt like a participant in *The Bachelorette*. No doubt the nurse had read the stupid article in a local publication that had named him the wealthiest and most eligible bachelor in Texas.

It amazed him what people posted in the name of entertainment.

They passed several partitions and had almost reached the fourth one when Durk had to step aside to permit a gurney guided by two paramedics to pass. The patient was muttering and fighting the restraints that kept her from propelling herself to the floor. Blood stained the white sheet.

Another nurse rushed over to meet them.

"We called ahead as soon as we got her on board," one of the paramedics explained. "Patient was attacked in her condo. She was unconscious when we got there and blood pressure is roller-coastering. A Taser was found on the premises. Not sure if it was used on her or not, but somebody's fists definitely were."

"Trauma unit is expecting her. Did she call for the ambulance before she blacked out?"

"No. A neighbor dialed 911. Apparently he heard her yell for help and went to her rescue. Huge guy with bulging muscles. Just the kind you want around when you need help. He took a couple of blows himself, but he refused to come in."

The gurney's occupant groaned and tried to sit up.

"You can relax. You're safe now," the nurse said. She walked beside the patient as they hurried off.

"Who's driving my car?" the woman asked.

"You're not in a car. You're in a hospital."

"Someone has to drive."

The voice was slurred, the tone bordering on delirious, yet the familiarity of it cut through Durk like a knife. He caught up with the gurney and caught a glimpse of the battered, confused patient. The right side of her face was red and swollen and her hair was matted with blood.

His insides rolled violently. "Meghan."

She showed no response. He reached for her hand. "It's Durk, Meghan."

"The car is going to wreck."

She was so out of it that she wasn't aware he was standing there, nor even where she was.

Pam caught up with him. "Do you know this woman?"

"I do."

"Are you related?" the other nurse asked.

"No, just friends."

"Then please stick around in case we need some information about her that she's not coherent enough to give."

He followed the gurney around the corner.

"You'll have to wait out here," the nurse said as they rolled Meghan through a set of double doors.

"I'd like to make sure she's okay."

"Someone will talk to you after she's been examined. There's nothing you can do now. She doesn't even know you're here."

He took a few steps back and then leaned against the wall while he struggled for a grip on reality.

Meghan Sinclair, the one woman he'd never been able to forget. Brutally attacked. So confused she didn't know where she was. Likely suffering from a concussion. Possibly much worse.

Durk had never sought vengeance before, but this was different. Whoever did this to Meghan would live to regret it. He would make damn sure of that.

Chapter Two

"They'll be awhile. Would you like to see your aunt now?"

Pam's question jerked Durk back to the situation that had brought him to the hospital in the first place. He nodded his agreement and followed her back down the hall, though his concern for Meghan didn't let up.

"How qualified is the trauma unit to handle head injuries?"

"We have one of the best in Dallas. Your friend is in good hands."

"Is there a neurologist on duty?"

"There is and several others they can call in if your friend's condition warrants it."

"Good."

"You seem very concerned. The patient must be a very close friend."

He let Pam's comment go without a response while he tried to deal with the emotions bucking inside him. It had been two years since he'd seen Meghan. But he doubted there had been a day since then that he hadn't thought about her. Not a night that he hadn't ached to hold her in his arms again.

He heard Sybil's voice even before they reached her curtained cubicle. She sounded a bit croaky, but her words were distinct.

Pam shoved the curtain back enough to peek inside. "You have a visitor, Mrs. Ratcliff."

"Who is it?"

"Your nephew, Durk Lambert."

"Durk. Really? My sister-in-law must be calling the whole family."

"He can come in," another female voice said.

Pam pushed back the curtain and ushered Durk inside. "I'll be back to check on you and your aunt in a bit," she said. "But don't leave before the trauma team can talk to you."

"No, I won't." That was a definite.

A female in a white doctor's coat looked up from the chart she was reading. "I'm Dr. Preston. And this is Bill Henley," she said, motioning to the nurse who was adjusting a blood pressure cuff on his aunt's arm. "We'll be looking after your aunt."

"Except that I don't need looking after," Sybil protested. "What I need is to go home."

"If you keep saying that, you're going to hurt my feelings," Bill teased.

"It's not you. In fact, you should go home with me," Sybil said. "A few days on the ranch and away from all these sick people would do you good."

"Amen to that," Bill agreed. "Where do I sign up?"

"As you can tell, she's feeling better," Dr. Preston said. "The good news is she didn't have a heart attack."

"That's a relief," Durk agreed.

"I never thought it was a heart attack," Sybil said. "But when I told Bessie I was having chest pains, she insisted on calling for an ambulance."

"Always better to err on the side of caution," Dr. Preston said. "Chest pains are nothing to fool around with."

Sybil nodded. "I lost my husband to a heart attack almost eleven years ago."

"I'm sorry." Dr. Preston handed the chart to Bill. "But that means you know how important cardiac care is."

Bill took the chart and left the room.

Durk stepped to the side of the bed, leaned over and gave his aunt a peck on the cheek. She looked a bit frail and her thick black wig had twisted on her head so that it looked as if it were trying to crawl away.

"When did the pains start?" Durk asked.

"About an hour ago."

"And you were feeling okay before that?"

"I haven't been feeling great the last few days, but I haven't really been sick, either—just tired and out of breath easily. Then, like I just explained to Dr. Preston, Bessie and I were walking to my car in the parking lot outside Neiman Marcus when all of a sudden I had stabbing pains in my chest. I told Bessie what was going on, and she called 911."

Durk turned to the doctor. "But you're sure that wasn't her heart?"

"No. I'm only sure she wasn't having a heart attack. The symptoms could have been caused by any number of things. We won't know for certain until we run some tests. Bill's arranging for those now."

"Pshaw. It was just indigestion," Sybil said. "I don't need any tests."

Durk took her hand in his. "I think we should leave that decision to Dr. Preston."

"A good plan," the doctor agreed.

"What kind of tests are we talking about?" Durk asked.

"I've ordered a chest X-ray and some blood

work for starters. Then we'll work from there until we can pinpoint the problem."

"I'm already feeling much better," Sybil insisted. She tried to sit up, but winced in pain and let her head fall back to the thin pillow.

"I won't have to stay the night, will I?" Sybil asked, though her tone was less argumentative than before.

"Why don't we decide that after I see the initial test results?"

Sybil nodded in agreement but she looked worried and her breathing seemed shallow even to Durk. Someone should probably stay with her, but he doubted it would be him. Any other time, he'd easily be up to the task, but seeing Meghan in that condition had him so shaken it was difficult to focus on anyone else.

"I'm going to step outside and call Mom," he said. "She made me promise to let her know how you were the second I saw you."

"Tell Carolina there's no use in her rushing up here. I'm fine," Sybil said. "And there's no reason for you to stay, either. I'm sure I can drive home."

"I'll give Mom that message." Which she'd immediately ignore. And then she'd question him about why his plans had changed and he wouldn't be coming to the ranch—at least not tonight.

Once he'd made the call to his mother and she'd declared she was on her way to the hospital, he walked back to the area where they'd taken Meghan. One of the nurses approached him.

"Are you here with the patient who was assaulted?"

"Meghan Sinclair?"

"Yes."

"I didn't come in with her, but she's a friend and I'm greatly concerned about her."

"Good. Hopefully you can help us. It's urgent that we get in touch with a family member."

Panic swept through him. "How serious is this?"

"Her condition is still being assessed, but she's unable to give us any medical history. We need to talk to someone who'll know if she has any allergies or other medical conditions we should be aware of. And we need a next of kin to make medical decisions until she is able to do that for herself. Do you know how to reach Ms. Sinclair's parents?"

"Her parents are dead."

"What about siblings?"

"She has a sister who lived in Connecticut," he said. "I assume she still lives there."

"Can you give us the sister's name and phone number?"

"Meghan called her Lucy. She's married, and I don't know her last name or her phone number. I'm sure Meghan's assistant, Ben Conroe, can give you everything you need."

"Do you have his phone number?"

"Not off hand, but I can get it. In fact, he needs to be notified. I know he'd want to be here."

"Would he also have her medical insurance information?"

"He'll at least know who holds the policy."

"Then have him contact us at this number ASAP." She handed him a business card for the trauma unit. "Tell him to ask for Jane. I'll be here until midnight."

"I'll get in touch with Ben," Durk said, "as soon as you give me the honest truth about Meghan's medical condition."

"I'm sorry, but since you're not a family member, the only information I can give you is that she's being treated."

Durk understood rules, but he'd never been too keen on following them. "I'm the only one here to make sure she's taken care of. You want me to cooperate, then do the same," he said.

It was a bluff. He'd cooperate and do what was best for Meghan no matter what they did or didn't tell him.

"Wait here," the nurse said. "I'll see what I can do."

A couple of minutes later, she returned with a man in a white physician's lab coat. The apprehension on the man's face as he stuck out his hand was anything but reassuring.

His handshake was firm as he introduced himself as Dr. Levy.

"I'm Durk Lambert, and I appreciate you talking to me."

"I understand you're a close friend of Ms. Sinclair," the doctor said, his voice matter-of-fact.

"Yes," Durk agreed even though it was an exaggeration. "How serious are her injuries? I mean, are we talking critical?"

"All I can tell you now is that her condition is being assessed."

"Exactly what does that entail?"

"Examination, routine neurological tests and a CAT scan."

"Is she conscious?"

"She's alert, but exhibiting altered mental status."

"What does that mean?"

"She's confused. That frequently goes along with a concussion. But we do need to contact a family member. That's the one thing you can do at this point to help your friend."

"I'll take care of that," Durk said. "In the meantime, I want to make certain that Meghan receives the best care possible, even if that means airlifting her to a different facility."

The doctor's brows arched. "At your expense?"

"Yes. I can sign whatever is needed."

"That's a very generous offer, Mr. Lambert, but there's no reason to move her at this time."

"In that case, when can I see her?"

"That depends on her progress and the test results, but likely within the next several hours. It will be good for her to hear a familiar voice—unless there's some reason why seeing you would upset her. There isn't, is there?"

"No."

"Then I'll let you know when you can see her."

Durk reconsidered his answer to that last question as he walked away. He and Meghan hadn't parted on the best of terms. Not that she'd made a scene. Meghan Sinclair was not one to lose control. But she'd clearly dumped him.

That had been two years ago. When he'd recommended her professional services to his brother Tague just months ago she'd accepted and done a bang-up job.

She'd moved on. For all he knew, she was in a serious romantic relationship. The thought bothered him, though it shouldn't. He'd bow out quickly enough if he found out that was true.

It wouldn't change the fact that he planned to make damn sure that whoever did this to Meghan would not get off scot-free.

But the first order of business was contacting Ben Conroe. He searched for a quiet space. When he found none, he walked outside and into the gathering twilight. The siren of an incoming ambulance punctuated the brisk air as he called Meghan's office.

He got a busy signal instead of the answering machine, and he breathed a sigh of relief. Hopefully, that meant Ben was still at work. The office was on the second floor of a three-story office building across the street from a strip mall only a few blocks away.

Durk jogged to his truck and a few seconds later was heading out of the parking lot. He dialed the number again as he sped toward her office. The line remained busy.

He glanced at his watch as he parked in the

mostly empty lot. It was ten before six. He entered and raced up the stairs to the second floor. He tapped on the closed door to her office. When no one answered, he pushed it open and stepped inside.

Ben was there, but he was not on the phone. He wouldn't be talking—not now and not ever again. A bullet had apparently ripped through his brain.

Durk went into defensive mode instantly, reaching for the pistol that lay near Ben's body, listening and looking for any sign the killer was still on the premises.

The office remained as quiet as death.

Feeling a bit more confident that he was alone, Durk stepped closer to the body. Ben's eyes were open, staring and lifeless. Durk stooped and checked Ben's pulse, knowing there wouldn't be one. The body was still warm. He'd missed the killer by mere minutes.

Reality burned in the pit of his stomach as he tried to assess the situation with some degree of clarity. Ben was dead. And whoever had killed him had probably planned the same fate for Meghan. Something had apparently stopped him before he could finish the job on her—possibly the neighbor who'd called the ambulance.

Fury and determination strained every mus-

cle as Durk took out his phone and dialed 911.
He gave the operator the information. She asked
a few questions, assured him the cops were on
their way and warned him not to touch anything
before they arrived.

A little late for that since he was likely already
holding the murder weapon. Survival topped
crime scene protocol any day. Too bad he hadn't
thought to grab his own pistol from the car, but
then he hadn't expected to crash a murder scene.

He let his gaze roam the small outer office.
File cabinet drawers were open, loose papers
strewn about the floor and across what had been
Ben's desk.

Gun still in hand, he crossed the room and,
using the tips of his fingers to hopefully keep
from destroying possible fingerprints, he cau-
tiously turned the knob and opened the door to
Meghan's office. The usually neat space was a
total wreck.

Whatever the murderous bastard had wanted,
Durk assumed he'd found it. Otherwise, he'd
have still been here when Durk showed up.

When the cops arrived, they'd take over. From
that point on, everything in the office would
be in their possession and Durk would be the
outsider—or possibly even a suspect since his

prints would be all over the Smith & Wesson still clutched in his right hand.

He'd deal with the suspicions, but the idea of losing control disturbed him to the max. The least he could do was locate the insurance information for the doctor so that they could check for a history of allergies.

He made his way to the ravaged file cabinet, stepping over scattered files and loose papers as best he could. Before he could locate the insurance file, the office phone rang. Durk answered quickly.

"Hello," the female voice responded. "Is Meghan around?"

"May I ask who's calling?"

"Lucy. Who is this?"

Durk's mouth went dry. Exactly who he needed to talk to, but he hated the news he had to deliver. "I'm a friend of Meghan's," he explained, working to keep his voice steady. "I'm afraid I have bad news, Lucy. There's been an incident."

"What kind of incident?"

"Meghan was attacked in her apartment this afternoon. She's in the hospital."

He heard the gasp and then the tremble in the voice. "Oh, no. How bad is she hurt?"

"They're running tests now to determine the seriousness of her condition."

"What hospital? I want to talk to her."

"Grantland, but she can't talk just yet. Her doctor is eager to hear from you, though. He needs to know if Meghan has any drug allergies that he should be aware of."

"Where's Ben? Is he with Meghan?"

Durk considered his answer. He hated to throw even more at Lucy when he knew so few facts. "Ben's not available, but I'll be with Meghan until she's out of danger."

"Who are you?"

"Durk Lambert. We've never met, but I'm a friend of Meghan's."

"Yes. I know who you are." Her tone told him she'd not only heard of him, but that he had at least two strikes against him in her book.

"How are you involved in this?" she demanded.

"By chance. I was at the emergency room checking on my aunt when Meghan was brought in. And it doesn't really matter what you think of me right now, Lucy. The only thing that matters is Meghan, and I promise you that I will see that she has the best of care. Right now you need to call Dr. Levy. Do you have a pen or pencil handy?"

"Wait."

He could hear her muffled voice talking to someone else. Thankfully, she wasn't alone. A few seconds later a male voice addressed him. "This is Johnny Delmar, Lucy's husband. Give me the doctor's phone number."

Durk did and then gave Johnny his number, as well. "I'd like permission to hire a private nurse around the clock if that seems warranted."

"I don't see any problems with that," Johnny said. "Except I'm sure Ben Conroe will see that Meghan has whatever she needs."

"That won't be possible."

"Why not? Doesn't Ben still work for Meghan?"

Durk hesitated, hating to get into a drawn-out explanation when the cops would arrive any second. But better that Johnny be there when Lucy heard about the murder. "You may as well know now as later. Ben's dead. He was shot in the head."

A few seconds of silence followed that pronouncement. "Were Ben and Meghan together?"

"No."

"What the hell is going on down there in Dallas?"

"I've told you all I know. I'm expecting the

cops any second, but right now Meghan's medical concerns top the priority list."

"Absolutely. We have a problem here, as well," Johnny said. "Lucy is going to want to catch the next flight to Texas, but she's eight months pregnant. She's having some complications and her obstetrician has ordered total bed rest until the delivery."

"Keep Lucy in Connecticut," Durk encouraged. "When I leave here, I'm going straight back to the hospital and I'll be there as long as Meghan is at risk. Count on it. I'll keep Lucy informed of everything."

"I'll see what I can do. But I'm not sure how much faith Lucy has in you."

"I understand that. But I still consider Meghan a friend. Nothing that happened between us changed that. I'll make certain Meghan gets the best of care."

Durk heard footsteps in the hallway. "I've got to go now. The cops are here."

He hung up the phone and walked into the outer office, leaving the murder weapon behind him on Meghan's desk.

"Hands over your head and face the wall," one

of the cops demanded. All weapons were drawn and pointed straight at him.

For once in his life, Durk followed orders without as much as a blink.

Chapter Three

Bearing a family name well-known in Dallas's social, business and philanthropic circles frequently offered significant perks and dismaying pitfalls. In this situation, it definitely worked to Durk's advantage.

The cops were actually giving him a chance to explain the circumstances instead of just hauling him off in a squad car to be interrogated at the local precinct.

He detailed every move he'd made since he'd first spotted Meghan at the hospital, giving particular attention to his actions at the crime scene. But even though they listened to his account, he wasn't sure they were convinced of his innocence.

"Check it out for yourselves," Durk said. "Talk to the cops who answered the 911 call to Meghan Sinclair's apartment. Talk to the E.R. staff at Grantland. They'll tell you I was there to see my aunt when they brought Meghan in and that Dr. Levy specifically requested that I help them gather needed medical and insurance information."

"And so you rushed to the office of a woman you admittedly hadn't seen for two years?"

"I figured her assistant was the best source of the information they needed. Like I said, I remembered she didn't have any family in the area."

One of the cops scratched a craggy jaw that was sporting a five o'clock shadow. "Wouldn't it have made more sense to call the assistant instead of rushing over here?"

"I did, but the line was busy. Besides, I figured this was the kind of news better delivered in person."

"How long has Mr. Conroe worked for Ms. Sinclair?"

"At least two years," Durk said. "Probably longer."

"Did Meghan mention any problems between her and Ben?"

"No, they appeared to be very close, but like I said, I haven't actually talked to Meghan in a couple of years."

"Yet here you are," one of the cops noted. "A

busy executive like you, rushing in to help an ex-girlfriend."

The sarcasm didn't warrant a response.

"Were Meghan and Ben romantically involved?" another cop asked.

"Not to my knowledge." At least they hadn't been two years ago. "As far as I know they were just coworkers and friends," he added, though he couldn't imagine what relevance a relationship between them would have to the case. It wasn't as if Meghan had shot him and then beat herself up.

But Meghan was going to take the news of Ben's murder hard. And knowing her, she'd be out looking for the killer the second she was released from the hospital—if not before.

A middle-aged cop with salt-and-pepper hair, a nose that showed signs of being broken more than once and a spare tire that hid his belt had asked most of the questions. His was the only name Durk had caught in the noisy confusion that accompanied their arrival. Officer Jordon.

Durk addressed his next question to him. "Do I need to contact my attorney or are you going to release me to return to the hospital and check on Meghan Sinclair?"

"First off, I need to request a crime scene unit. Then I'll make a few calls to verify your story.

If everything checks out, you're free to go—for the time being. However, I expect you'll be contacted shortly by a detective. Are you staying in town for the Thanksgiving holiday?"

"Yes, I'll either be at my home or at the hospital. And you can assure the detective I'll be glad to help in any way I can. If he thinks a reward will help flush out the perpetrator, I'll supply the funds."

Durk waited while Officer Jordon made the calls, his mind struggling to make sense of the attack and murder. Had the killer come to the office first, killed Ben and then gone after Meghan?

Had he gone to both places looking for something in particular—like files on one of her cases? Had he found them, or had Bill Mackey frightened him away before he could fully search her condo?

Or was this someone Meghan had helped put away coming back to exact revenge?

At this point, those were all merely theories. Hopefully when Meghan was talking again, she'd be able to explain everything and identify the man who'd assaulted her and killed Ben.

Assuming they were one and the same.

Fortunately, the officer's calls backed up everything Durk had told them. Once released,

Durk made a quick exit before the CSU team arrived.

On his way to the car, he called the number the nurse named Jane had given him. As soon as he identified himself, she thanked him for having Lucy call them but still refused to release any information on Meghan.

He figured Pam might be more accommodating, but when he got her on the phone, all she could tell him was that his aunt was being admitted to the hospital for observation and further tests.

Which meant Durk would undoubtedly run into his mother before the night was over. She'd be a much tougher interrogator than the cops had been as to his involvement with Meghan.

One thing you could always count on as a Lambert: your secrets never stayed that way for long. Not that he had any reason to hide his past relationship with Meghan. They had been lovers for a while and then they weren't.

The past was simple. The feelings churning inside him now were inextricably complicated.

Durk made a stop at his penthouse condo to take a quick shower and change from his bloody dress clothes into a pair of jeans, a blue pullover shirt and his boots.

He also took a couple of over-the-counter

painkillers. What had started as a dull ache while he was still at the scene of the crime had burgeoned into a hammering throb at both temples.

By the time he made it back to the hospital, stars and a crescent moon were shining in the night sky. Not that they ever sparkled inside the Dallas city limits with the same brilliance as they did on the ranch.

It dawned on him as he parked that he'd never taken Meghan to the Bent Pine Ranch.

He climbed from behind the wheel and walked to the E.R. entrance, hoping to dodge interference and make his way back to the trauma unit on his own.

No such luck. Pam spotted him as he walked through the door. She waved from behind the glass partition and motioned him over to where she was talking to a patient.

"Give me a minute to finish here and I'll be right with you," she chirped. She looked back to her patient and handed the woman a clipboard. "Just fill this out while you're waiting and sign the areas that are highlighted. Bring it back to the desk when you finish."

As the woman walked away, Pam turned her full attention back to Durk. "I have a break due, so I can show you to your aunt's room."

"Actually, I was going to check on Meghan Sinclair first."

She frowned. "I wouldn't recommend it."

"Why not?"

"There's a detective from the DPD waiting to talk to her. I expect he'll get first dibs when the doctor says she's up for visitors. And if you're hanging around back there, he'll likely question you, as well."

"I'll take my chances," Durk said. "But thanks for the warning." He smiled and walked away before she could join him.

Durk found Jane in the E.R. nurse's station arguing with a tall man in jeans and a tan-colored sport coat. The guy looked to be in his early forties and easily as tall as Durk's six-foot-two-inch frame. Hard body. Craggy, tan face. Thick sandy-colored hair that looked as if it had been held in place with a glue gun.

Jane looked up, her expression flashing relief when she saw Durk. "Here's Mr. Lambert now." She motioned Durk over. "This detective has been looking for you."

"Has there been any change in Meghan's condition?" Durk asked.

"All I can tell you at this point is that she's being seen by the trauma medical staff, the same as I told Detective Sam Smart here. Now if you'll both excuse me, I need to get back to nursing. That is what they pay me for."

"I still need to talk to Ms. Sinclair the minute she's able," the detective said to her back as she walked away.

Jane didn't respond.

The detective stared at Durk as if he were sizing him up for a new suit—or a fight. Durk figured he was going for intimidation. It didn't work. He was a master at that himself.

"Glad to run into you here," the detective said. "It will save me a trip to your house."

"Is this concerning Meghan's attack or her assistant's murder?"

"Both."

"So you're in homicide?"

"Exactly."

"You didn't waste any time getting started on the case," Durk said.

"Time is seldom on a detective's side in a murder case. So let's talk."

"Talk or interrogate me?"

Sam shrugged his shoulders. "Is there a difference?"

"Quite a bit. If you want facts, I can tell you the little I know. If you're going to interrogate me as a suspect, I should call my attorney."

"I'm just after the facts—unless, of course, you have something to confess."

"I already confessed to handling the possible murder weapon." And he had nothing to hide. Unfortunately, he had nothing of any real value to add, either. If and when he needed an attorney, he'd get the best in the business. He didn't see it going that far, especially since Meghan would vouch that he wasn't her attacker.

Durk stuck his hands in the front pockets of his jeans. "So do we talk here in the middle of the noisy hallway or do you want to try for something a bit more private?"

Smart smirked. "Are you worried about being seen with a homicide detective?"

"Just trying to be helpful," Durk said.

"I'm glad you feel that way."

The detective led the way to a back exit. They stepped outside but didn't venture away from the building.

Smart propped his shoulder against the wall. "How well do you know Meghan?"

"Reasonably well. We dated for several months two years ago."

"Then I assume you're aware of what she does for a living?"

"I know she's a private investigator," Durk admitted.

"She specializes in cases involving extremely dangerous criminals, the kind of cases best left to trained police officers."

"And I hear she's good at it," Durk said. "So, what's your point?"

"The point is that you'd be smart not to get involved in this case other than cooperating with me and the rest of the DPD."

In other words, butt out. Durk had a real problem with ultimatums—unless he was the one issuing them. "What makes you think I'd get involved?"

"You might look like a cowboy, but I know all about you, Durk. You're a powerful CEO. You're used to being in charge and running things your way."

"I'm noted for getting the job done, just like Meghan."

"But you're not used to dealing with murderers. Take it from me, they don't play by any rules. This guy has killed once. He won't hesitate to do it again if that's what it takes to save his skin."

"I plan to stay alive," Durk said. "With or without rules."

The groundwork of their tenuous relationship had been laid. The rest of the detective's questions were routine and the interview was over as soon as the detective realized that Durk knew nothing about the cases Meghan was currently working.

When Smart left, Durk walked back inside. Jane met up with him right away.

"Dr. Levy would like to speak with you."

Now they were getting somewhere. "When?"

"As soon as he has a minute. If you'll wait near the trauma unit nurse's station, I'll come for you when he's ready."

Jane's voice had taken on a somber tone that set his nerves on edge.

"I'll be there," he said. Waiting. Worrying. Agonizing over what Dr. Levy would have to say and unable to do one thing to change it.

"Ms. Sinclair is exhibiting symptoms of a severe brain concussion."

Durk breathed easier at Dr. Levy's pronouncement. He was familiar with concussions, having experienced two of them while playing quarterback for the Oak Grove Wildcats. But his had been mild, and the only symptoms he remembered were a headache and vomiting all over his uniform.

"What symptoms?" he asked.

"She lost consciousness for several minutes during her exam and she is experiencing AMS—

altered mental status. In Ms. Sinclair's case she's combative, pushing the medical team away when we try to examine her. She keeps yelling about being in a car wreck."

"She was doing that when they brought her in," Durk recalled.

"She's also unable to answer simple questions or state her name."

"Is that normal with a severe concussion?"

"It's not unusual, especially immediately following the trauma."

"Can you give her something to help her focus?"

"We don't want to give her any meds at this point. Drugs would affect her neurological functioning and we want to keep a close check on those for the next few hours."

"Exactly what do you mean when you say neurological functioning? Are there other injuries?"

"She has a relatively small hematoma behind her right ear and two cuts in her scalp that will need to be sutured. But nothing else to be concerned about."

"What about her blood pressure? The paramedic mentioned that it was roller-coastering when they rolled her in."

"That was most likely the result of having

been Tasered. We're monitoring that. It shouldn't present a continuing problem."

"And that's it? No life-threatening injuries?"

"That's all we know at this time. We're in the process of scheduling a CT scan to see if there are other issues."

Durk's apprehension climbed again. He was fairly certain that CT scans were not the norm for a concussion. "You must have noticed some indicator that this could possibly be more severe than a concussion?"

Dr. Levy pushed his small-rimmed glasses up the bridge of his nose. "You're very perceptive, Mr. Lambert."

"But not particularly medically astute," Durk said. "Still, I get the feeling that you're not totally convinced that the concussion is the worst of Meghan's condition."

"In truth, I might have ordered a CT scan in this case just because of the severity of the concussion. But your assumption is correct. One of our residents noticed a small bruise, sometimes referred to as a battle sign, behind Ms. Sinclair's right ear during the examination. It can indicate a fracture to the skull. It's something we need to check out."

"Then it's still a matter of wait and see?"

"For now. If you'll leave your cell phone number with Jane, I'll call you when we know more."

"Good, because I won't be leaving the hospital until I hear from you." If then. "But why this sudden decision to share Meghan's medical information with a nonfamily member?"

"Lucy Delmar got back to us immediately. She gave us the information we needed and faxed us a release form with your name included. I can't thank you enough for your help with that."

"Thanks." So Lucy had come through for him. He had an idea that her husband had convinced her to do that. He'd make sure he thanked him, as well. And he'd make a point of keeping in touch with them until Meghan was fully recovered.

He had to believe that would be soon. It was the only way he could face this without having his own spell of AMS.

Sitting and waiting had never been his style, but this time he didn't have a choice.

When Dr. Levy left, Durk gave his cell number to Jane and then tracked Pam down again. Armed with his aunt's room number, he made his way to the elevator.

A few hours ago, he'd been anticipating a week's vacation at the ranch with nothing more challenging on his plate than deciding whether to take a sunrise horseback ride or sleep until noon.

Now he had a murder to contend with and a detective that clearly wasn't convinced of his innocence. Yet all Durk could think about was Meghan Sinclair. If he wasn't careful, he'd be exactly where he was two years ago.

His heart couldn't take that again.

SAM SMART PACED the E.R. hallway, racking his brain to figure out how and why Durk Lambert had ended up at a murder scene. Not only was he CEO of Lambert Inc., but his family owned the oil and gas company, along with the Bent Pine Ranch and several smaller subsidiaries related to drilling operations.

Having accidentally encountered Meghan as she was being wheeled into the E.R. didn't explain his actions, especially when he hadn't even seen her in two years. There had to be something Sam was missing here.

Not that Meghan wasn't the kind of woman who could get under a man's skin and make him do crazy things. She was spunky, analytical, insightful. Not to mention incredibly sexy.

She'd have made a great homicide detective had she chosen to play by cop rules. Instead she was the frequent bane of the DPD, usurping their authority and making them look incompetent.

Sam had tangled with her himself on more than one occasion. And, yeah, he'd experienced a few pangs of lust while trying and failing to best her.

But a man like Durk Lambert had gorgeous socialites at his beck and call. Hell, the man had probably been in and out of bed with dozens of young hotties in the past two years. Not that Sam faulted him for that. He'd have done the same had he been in Durk's shoes—or boots as was the case now.

That was another thing that concerned Sam. The cops had described the bloody clothes Durk was wearing when they encountered him at Meghan's office. Expensive clothing, the kind a wealthy oil executive would be expected to wear.

Yet now he'd shown up at the hospital dressed like an everyday cowboy. Faded jeans. Goat-roper Western boots. A knit pullover shirt that could have come off the rack at any department store in Dallas.

If Durk was trying to give the impression that he was just a good old boy out to help a friend, Sam wasn't buying it. Yet his story about visiting his aunt had been true. Sam had wasted no time checking that out.

He doubted Durk was the loyal friend he played at being, but that was not a good enough reason to blame the night's violence on him.

But you could never be sure. Men with the kind of assets and power that Durk possessed had a tendency to believe they were above the law.

Maybe Durk had been trying to get back into the saddle with Meghan and discovered that Ben had replaced him. He could have fought with her and then killed Ben. The story about Durk's handling the murder weapon for his own protection could be just a clever cover-up.

But that was a long shot at best. Meghan Sinclair had countless enemies, dangerous criminals who'd thought they were home free until she showed up. The list of suspects with motives to get back at her was practically endless.

He figured they were looking at just one suspect for both crimes, but he'd keep an open mind about that. Anyway you called it, his best bet at catching their killer would be for Meghan to identify her attacker.

But would she?

Or would she choose to bypass the police and go after the bastard herself? Sam planned to make damn sure she didn't. He would not be outsmarted by her. Not again.

DURK TAPPED ON the door to Sybil's hospital room, and his mother whispered for him to come in. Sybil was sound asleep, snoring, her jaw slack. She was almost unrecognizable without the infernal black wig plastered to her head.

"How is she?" he whispered.

"They've diagnosed her with pleurisy." His mother stood and tiptoed toward him. "Let's talk in the hall. She needs her rest."

They stepped outside the room, softly closing the door behind them.

"I feel like I'm getting a crash course in medicine tonight. Isn't pleurisy some kind of respiratory ailment?"

"Yes, basically. The E.R. doctor described it as an inflammation of the lining of the lungs and chest."

"Is it serious?"

"It can be. But in Sybil's case, the doctor expects it to respond to antibiotics. They gave her an injection so that it could start working at once. If she's feeling better, she'll go home in the morning and can follow up with her regular doctor."

"You're not going to try and stay with her all night, are you?" he asked.

"I'm thinking about it."

"That doesn't get my vote. Not only will you

be sore from sitting in that chair all night, but you won't get any sleep. You'll need your rest tonight if you're going to take care of Sybil tomorrow."

"I'll have plenty of help from Emma and Alexis once I get her home. Your two sisters-in-law will both pitch in."

"Spend the night at my place," he urged. "All the comforts of home."

"I suppose I could stay in your guest room and then drive back to the hospital in the morning."

"Great idea. Don't know why I didn't think of it myself," he teased. "You'll have the place to yourself and won't have Grandma Pearl turning the volume on the TV up to deafening decibels. Do you have your key with you?"

"I do. If you're not going to be at home, does that mean you're driving out to the ranch tonight?"

"No, and probably not tomorrow, either." No reason not to level with her except that he dreaded having to explain a relationship with Meghan that he didn't fully understand himself.

Carolina pushed a lock of graying hair behind her ear. "I'm assuming this has to do with the emergency you mentioned earlier."

He nodded.

She frowned and pulled her gold-colored

cardigan tight around her chest. "You're letting that oil company take over your life, Durk. You haven't had a real vacation in months. You have a nephew, a foster niece and two new sisters-in-law you've barely met. Whatever it is, can't you just delegate it to someone else this time?"

He smiled in spite of his worries. He might be thirty years old and a CEO, but that didn't keep his mother from tearing into him if she thought he needed it. No matter how high up the corporate level he climbed or how old he got, he was still her kid.

"This has nothing to do with business, Mom. I have a friend who's in the hospital and I'm staying in town to make sure she's okay."

"She?"

More reason he hated going there with his mother, the matchmaker. "Just a friend, Mom."

"Do I know her?"

"Meghan Sinclair."

Her brows arched. "Isn't that the private detective who worked with Tague and Alexis when that horrible man was trying to kill Alexis?"

"That's the one."

"I'm so sorry. I know Alexis really liked her. Did she have surgery?"

"Not yet, and hopefully she won't have to. She

was the victim of a brutal attack tonight when she was returning to her condo."

"Oh, no. Will she be all right?"

"I hope so." And now he might as well tell her the rest since she'd hear it all on the morning news and so would his brothers.

Shock registered in every line of her face as he went over the details of his finding Ben Conroe's body. By the time he finished, her eyes were wet with unshed tears.

"Poor Meghan. She'll have so much to face and no family here to see her through this. Of course you should stay with her. Just..." Anxiety shook her voice. "Just don't get involved in the murder case, son. Leave that to the cops. Please."

He put his arms around her shoulder. "I have no intention of becoming a vigilante, Mom." That was the most he could promise.

"Why don't you go to my place now, Mother? There's no reason to just sit around and watch Aunt Sybil sleep. I'll stick around awhile in case she wakes up, but she looks as if she's out for the night. And if she wakes up and needs something, I'll only be an elevator ride away."

"Very well. I'll give your phone number to the nursing staff."

"And take that god-awful wig with you so

that it doesn't frighten the nurses away during the night."

"I'm not about to take the wig. Heaven forbid Sybil wakes up in the morning and has to face her doctor without it."

His mother gathered her things and kissed his sleeping aunt on the cheek. He walked her to his car and then grabbed a cup of coffee from the hospital café before going back to his aunt's room.

Time dragged by and he'd almost dozed off when his cell phone vibrated. He yanked it from his pocket and rushed into the hall to take the call.

"This is Jane, in E.R. Can you come back to our nursing station, Mr. Lambert? Dr. Levy has the reports back from Ms. Sinclair's scan and he'd like to discuss the results with you."

His uneasiness swelled to a sickening dread as he rushed back to the elevator to face whatever news was waiting for him.

Chapter Four

Durk followed Jane to a small conference room that held a metal table and a few hard folding chairs. Dr. Levy sat in one of the chairs, a mug of coffee at his elbow while he made notes on a patient chart.

He motioned for Durk to take a seat.

Durk remained standing. He thought best on his feet. "Did the scan show any skull fractures?" he asked, though he wasn't sure he was ready to hear the answer.

"No, the scan was negative for any type of brain injury."

Durk took a deep breath and exhaled slowly as he slid into the chair. "Can I see her?"

"You can."

Durk's hands grew clammy as anticipation and anxiety waged a choking battle inside him. Two long years of fighting the memories and trying to convince himself that he and Meghan had made the only decision that made sense and now he was about to insinuate himself right back in her life. Had he totally lost his mind?

He forced himself to focus on the doctor's words. Meghan had been moved to a private room in a telemetry unit so that her vital signs could be closely monitored. She was still in a state of confusion. She couldn't name the president of the United States or even state her own address or her phone number.

The doctor assured him the altered mental status was temporary and not unusual following a concussion. What she needed most from Durk was a calm, assuring, familiar voice.

Problem was that by the time he left the doctor and took the elevator to the telemetry unit, the memories were playing so much havoc with his emotions that he was anything but calm. Losing Meghan had been a hundred times more difficult than he'd imagined. She'd stalked his mind at times when he'd have least expected, haunted his dreams, made every woman he'd dated since seem sensually lame by comparison.

A nurse stopped at his elbow, interrupting his reverie. "Can I help you?"

"I'm here to visit Meghan Sinclair."

"You must be Durk Lambert. One of the nurses from the trauma unit just called. She said you were a close friend of the patient and that you were on your way up."

She opened the door to Meghan's room. *Ready or not,* he thought as he stepped inside. A chilling lump settled in his chest as he stopped next to the hospital bed and stared down at Meghan.

Her eyes were closed. One side of her face was swollen. The hematoma Dr. Levy had mentioned was the size of a walnut. Her head was bandaged where she'd had the sutures.

She looked incredibly frail and much younger than her thirty-one years. He covered her left hand with his. It was cool to the touch and unresponsive.

A flare of dark fury rushed through his veins. If he could just get his hands on the man who did this to her....

He muttered a curse and dropped to a chair next to the bed.

Meghan jerked and groaned without opening her eyes. Durk leaned in close. "You're safe, Meghan," he whispered softly. "You're going to be all right."

If she heard him, she gave no sign. His mind drifted back to the night they'd first met. At the last minute he'd let his mother, who had been ill with a stomach virus, talk him into attending a fundraiser in her place. It was one of her pet charities, an organization dedicated to helping pay medical expenses for physically handicapped children needing surgery.

He'd been in stressful meetings all day and had gone to the gala with plans to deliver her speech thanking all the donors for their contributions and then immediately cut out.

But then he'd spotted Meghan Sinclair across the room and become totally intrigued. She was stunning in an emerald-green ball gown and a crown of the most gorgeous red silky hair he'd ever seen.

But the real fascination came from the impact of watching her flip her wrist and empty a crystal flute of champagne in the face of his least favorite Texas politician. Durk had no doubt that the jerk deserved it.

Durk had made a point of meeting her after that incident and ended up driving her home and staying for breakfast—two days in a row. He'd never fallen so hard, so fast—not since Ellie Jenkins had kissed him in the sixth grade.

His thoughts shifted from the past to the here and now. Meghan was in the hospital, confused and battered. Ben Conroe was lying in a morgue. And somewhere a killer was going on with his life.

Eventually Durk must have dozed off because

the next time he looked at his watch, it was an hour later. He stood, stretched and went to the bathroom. He relieved himself, washed his face in cold water and went in search of coffee.

After he finished the cup of strong brew, he slipped quietly back into Meghan's room. Only this time, Meghan's eyes were open wide and she was staring at the ceiling. She moaned as he approached the bed.

"Are you in pain?" he asked. "Should I get the nurse?"

She turned and looked at him, then closed her eyes again.

"Can I get you anything?" he repeated.

Still no response, but he was almost certain she was awake.

He sat and stayed quiet until she squirmed and began to rub her left hand. Then he stood and moved close to the bed.

"Is there anything you want to tell me?" he asked, sure that if she were fully conscious, she'd have questions about the attack.

She shuddered and finally met his gaze, staring at him as if he'd interrupted something important.

"Who are you and why are you in my bedroom?"

Chapter Five

Meghan stared into the deep, dark eyes of the cowboy who was standing over her. Him, the bed she was in, the noises and smells around her, all merged into a surreal sensation, as if she were drowning in a murky pond.

Images were vague—undefined and unfamiliar. Voices were indistinct. Her body didn't seem connected to her brain. Worse, a sense of panic overrode every other emotion.

"Who are you?" she asked again.

He looked almost as perplexed as she felt. "Am I that easy to forget, Meghan?"

What had he called her? Meghan? But her name was… She drew a foggy blank. How could she not know her own name?

She looked around and her thoughts coalesced enough that she realized she was in a hospital—or a nightmare. She stared at the rails on the side of the bed before finally looking back to the stranger.

"Should I know you?"

His gaze intensified and his expression grew strained. "Durk. I'm Durk Lambert, Meghan. We're friends."

There was a hazy familiarity about him, something that made her breath catch in her throat. "What happened? How did I get here?"

"Don't you remember?"

"No," she said, the admittance adding a new swell of anxiety.

"You were attacked."

"When was that?"

"Earlier tonight. In your condo. Your neighbor, Bill Mackey, heard your scream and came to your rescue. He chased your assailant away and called for an ambulance."

An attack. That explained why she felt as if heavy weights were attached to every muscle. She tried to bring her memories into focus. She couldn't picture her condo and had no idea who Bill Mackey was.

"Who attacked me? And why?"

"I was hoping you could answer those questions."

She closed her eyes and tried to pull facts from the dense fog that had settled in her brain.

The harder she tried, the more confused she became.

Frustrated, she opened her eyes again. Had her brain been damaged in the attack? Was that why she couldn't even remember her own name?

Her mouth grew dry. She couldn't swallow. A shudder ripped through her. "I want to see the doctor. I want to see him *now.*"

The man who called himself Durk pushed her call button, a task she could have done herself had she not switched to panic mode.

"Try to stay calm, Meghan. Everything's under control. You're in excellent hands."

"Everything is not fine. Don't lie to me."

"You're right. It's not fine yet, but it will be. You have a concussion, but you're getting the best care possible. You just need a little time to regain your memory and the ability to think clearly."

"How do you know that?"

"I made it my business to find out."

This cowboy with the penetrating gaze had taken control, as if she were his responsibility. As if she were his sister—or his wife. No, surely she'd recognize her husband even in her befuddled state.

Or would she? She didn't even recognize her

name. "Tell me," she said, hating this feeling of helplessness. "Exactly how do I know you?"

He put a hand over her bruised one. "We're friends, Meghan. Just friends. But I'm here to help in any way I can."

A nurse padded into the room in her thick, cushioned white shoes.

"She's awake," Durk said, speaking for her as if she wasn't there.

"That's great." The nurse smiled and put a cool hand on Meghan's arm. "I'm Angela Drake. I've been taking care of you—along with Durk. You're lucky to have a friend like him."

She'd decide if she was lucky, once she remembered him. "I want to talk to my doctor."

"I'll call him, but it may take him a while to get up here. He's involved with another emergency now. In the meantime, I'm here. Are you in pain?"

"My thoughts are muddled. I can't seem to remember anything."

Angela patted her shoulder. "Confusion is understandable after what you've been through."

"It's more than confusion. I'm… I don't remember being attacked or how I got here."

"Give yourself time. Just try to relax, Meghan. Let us do the worrying."

Meghan pushed her hair from her face. When

she tried to tuck it behind her ear, she felt a tender knot. She examined the rest of her head with her fingertips and discovered a bandage at the back, a few inches up from the base of her skull.

"Why is my head bandaged?"

"The doctor will explain everything to you and answer all your questions."

"Then please get him," Meghan pleaded.

"He'll be here soon," the nurse assured her. She lifted Meghan's right hand. "While we're waiting, can you squeeze my hand?"

Meghan squeezed, but her irritation was growing.

"Very good. Now squeeze a little harder."

Meghan squeezed even though it intensified what had been a dull ache at both temples.

Angela dropped her hand, pulled a flashlight from her pocket and shone a beam into Meghan's left eye and then her right.

"Do you know where you are, Meghan?"

"In a hospital."

Angela grinned as if Meghan had given the winning answer in a quiz show. "Do you remember how you got here?"

That question was tougher. Had Durk driven her here? No. He'd just told her. She waded through the haze.

She'd been attacked. There had been a rescue. A neighbor...

"I came by ambulance," she said, though she didn't remember being in one. All she knew was what Durk had just told her.

"Good for you, Meghan. You're coming around. I'll let Dr. Levy know you want to see him."

When Angela walked away, Meghan looked back at Durk, searching his face and especially his eyes, futilely hoping for some grain of recognition. There was nothing.

Durk leaned over her bed. "If my being here is upsetting you, I can leave. Is that what you want me to do?"

Yes. If she were by herself, she wouldn't have to think.

But right now he was her only link to her past, even if she didn't remember him. But he surely hadn't bargained for this when he'd come for a visit.

"Do you want to leave?" she asked.

"I want to do whatever makes you the most comfortable. But I won't go far, not until you're up and bossing us all around. Trust me, that won't take long."

"In that case, I'd like you to stay."

He took her hand. "I'll stay as long as you'll let me. And that's a promise."

She fought back tears. She was bewildered and afraid, but at least she wasn't alone. Her eyelids grew heavy in spite of the apprehension churning inside her.

As soon as she closed them, the drowning sensation returned, this time even stronger than before. The swirling water pulled her to the bottom.

As the breath escaped her lungs, a strong hand reached out to her. She held on tight and the cowboy pulled her to shore.

"HELLO, MEGHAN. I heard you wanted to talk to me."

Another stranger had wandered into her dream. She tasted fear and reached for the stranger who'd pulled her to safety. Her arms came up empty.

"It's Dr. Levy, Meghan. You're safe. Open your eyes and I'll answer all your questions."

Dr. Levy. She fought her way back through the haze. This time when she opened her eyes she turned first to see if the cowboy was there or if he'd only been in her dream.

But he was there, standing next to the bed, his gaze fixed on her.

"Good morning, sleeping beauty. Your doctor is here."

"Just as you requested," a smiling nurse added.

She looked at the window. No light crept through the blinds. "Is it morning?"

"It's three o'clock."

"You're Durk," she said as the images and her thoughts slowly came into focus.

"Yes, I am, and this is Dr. Levy and Angela."

She studied both of them. Only the nurse looked familiar.

"I hear you have lot of questions for me," Dr. Levy said. "But maybe I can clear up some of what's happened before you have to ask. Would you like for Angela to help you go to the bathroom before we get started?"

Now that he mentioned it, she did need to go. The prospect of getting her arms and legs coordinated made the task seem daunting even with Angela's help.

"It's only a few steps away," Dr. Levy said, as if reading her mind. "I'll tell you what, Durk and I will chat in the hallway and give you some privacy. Angela will let us know when you're back in bed."

"I need the answer to one question first," she said. "Do I have brain damage?"

"No, you have a significant concussion that's left you temporarily confused, a condition called retrograde amnesia. But your vital signs are good, as are your neuro signs other than the mental confusion. There's absolutely no indication of any permanent damage."

She took a deep breath and let the relief flood through her body. "That's what I needed to hear," she said. "But I do still have a few questions."

"That's a good sign," Dr. Levy said.

Durk took her hand and squeezed it gently before he left the room with the doctor. She could learn to like that man—if she ever figured out who he was.

Angela took it slowly with her, having her sit up and then dangle her legs over the side of the bed for a good minute before progressing to standing. She was a bit shaky, but wasn't nearly as unsteady as she'd feared.

Once she was erect, her thoughts seemed to clear a bit, though she still couldn't get her mind around exactly why she was in this hospital.

"Just lean on me," Angela encouraged her, "and we'll take it slowly. Are you dizzy?"

"Not really dizzy," she said, trying to be accurate. "I'm just a little unsteady."

"You're doing fine." Angela led her to the bathroom.

Meghan stopped at the mirror and stared at the image looking back at her. The right side of her face was swollen and bruised. Her hair looked as if it had been sucked into a cement mixer. The knot she'd felt behind her left ear made her head look lopsided.

Her insides churned. "Now I'm dizzy," she said. "And mortified. I look like a sun-baked alien."

"The assailant did a number on you," Angela said. "But give it a little time and the bruising and swelling will fade and you'll be the Meghan of old."

The Meghan of old. The Meghan she couldn't remember. Even if they were friends, it was amazing the handsome cowboy hadn't taken one look at her last night and run away screaming.

"Once your hair grows out, you won't even be able to see where the staples were."

"When my hair grows out?"

"They had to shave the area that required surgical staples to close the cuts."

So now she'd have bald spots in the middle of the back of her head. How much worse could this get?

Holding on to the basin with one hand, she turned on the water with the other and slid her hand beneath the cool flow. She splashed some on her face and then dabbed a bit onto her bangs. She smoothed the worst of the wild mass as best she could.

"I'll help you get cleaned up later," Angela offered. "Though you can't shampoo the hair yet. But right now we should let you talk to Dr. Levy."

Meghan murmured her agreement and gratefully looked away from the mirror. She pushed thoughts of her looks aside as she finished up in the bathroom and with Angela's help climbed back in the bed.

She had bigger concerns to deal with. Like where her memory had gone and who had attacked her and why. She didn't know about the old Meghan, but she wasn't going to take this lying down.

At least not once she could stand on her own two feet without assistance.

"HER NEUROLOGIST SAYS that temporary memory loss is common after a severe concussion," Durk explained to his brother Damien over a poor phone connection. "Loss of memory of events that happened immediately before or after the injury or within a few hours either way of the event."

"So Meghan doesn't remember anything before the attack?" Damien questioned.

"I wish that were it. At this point, she has complete loss of memory before last night. She didn't even recognize her own name at first."

"Then she doesn't remember you?"

"That's right, and that might be better for the time being. I've told her we're friends but haven't mentioned that we were ever more than that or that we haven't spoken in two years. By the way, I haven't mentioned to Mother that we were ever more than friends, either. Let's leave it that way for now."

"Isn't Mother sitting beside you now?"

"She's gone to refill our coffee cups."

Durk shifted the phone to his other ear. He'd just gone through all of this with her over breakfast in the hospital cafeteria. But when Damien had called, she'd handed her phone over to Durk to supply the pertinent details to him about what was going on with Meghan.

As expected, his mother had already shared the facts surrounding the attack and murder with both of his brothers. Not that he minded. If she hadn't, he would have. He and his brothers had always been there for each other when there was a problem.

And this was one hell of a problem.

Besides, both of his brothers had met Meghan when, at Durk's recommendation, Tague had hired her to help in an investigation. Meghan had impressed the hell out of them. Durk's new sister-in-law had been awed by her abilities, and the women had bonded immediately. For all Durk knew, they might have stayed in contact with each other.

He'd definitely check that out just in case Meghan had said something to Alexis that might give him some insight into the crimes.

"Is the doctor certain the amnesia is temporary?" Damien asked.

"He seems convinced that there's no permanent physical reason for the memory loss. But, as he said, emotional issues can also be a factor, and they're much more difficult to predict."

"Does Meghan know her assistant was murdered?"

"I haven't told her. I didn't figure she needed that kind of emotional trauma when she doesn't even know there was an assistant or what he assisted her in doing."

"Does that mean she hasn't been questioned by the police?"

"Not yet, but Detective Sam Smart has been assigned to head up the murder case. He looks like a playboy who needs a makeover, but he barks like a bulldog. He won't let the doctor keep him away long."

"Does the detective have any leads?"

"None that he's shared with me," Durk admitted. "I haven't talked to him today, though I'm sure I'm still on his radar."

"Why are you on his radar?"

Durk explained the situation.

"Having your fingerprints on the murder weapon is no laughing matter, Durk. You need to get a lawyer."

"On the *possible* murder weapon. And here comes Mother with our refill," he said, cuing Damien that it was time for a change in subject matter. "But I'll give your suggestion some thought."

"You should. How is Meghan doing other than the memory problems?"

"Her physical recovery is going great."

"And Meghan's sister is okay with you taking over this way?"

"I think Lucy is just relieved to have someone who cares about Meghan on top of things."

"And you're that someone?"

"No one else has stepped up to the plate."

"No current boyfriend?"

"Haven't heard from one as yet," Durk admitted, though there was no reason to think Meghan wasn't dating. But if there was a significant other, he figured Lucy would have mentioned him when he'd called her earlier this morning to thank her for adding his name to the privacy forms.

"So what's your next move?" Damien asked.

"I'm definitely staying in Dallas until Meghan rebounds and will probably spend most of my time at the hospital today. The nurse ran me out of the ward while Meghan gets showered and cleaned up. But I told the doctor that I want to be there when Meghan has to talk to Detective Smart. That will likely be later today."

"Tague has to come into Dallas on business this morning," Damien said. "He'll likely stop by the hospital. And I'm available, too, if there's anything I can do to help."

"I don't know what it would be unless you have a suggestion for a way to jog Meghan's memory."

"What about pictures? Do you have any snapshots that you took when the two of you were dating?"

None that he hadn't put through the shredder. Getting over Meghan had been difficult enough without having those around to torment him.

"No snapshots," he said.

"Meghan must have some at her condo. Pictures of her with friends, her sister, probably even some that go back a few years. They might help. Do you have a key to her condo?"

"Actually, I do." Not that he'd ever expected to use it again. "Thanks for the input, bro. I think I will stop by the condo and see what I can come up with."

"Better check with Detective Smart before you visit the crime scene, especially now that the attack is connected to a murder."

"Asking permission always runs the risk of hearing 'no.'"

"Not that you'd ever let a word stop you."

"No, but giving Smart a reason to arrest me doesn't seem the best way to start the day."

"Nor does getting involved in a murder in any way. Finding the perp is the detective's job. Just keep that in mind, Durk."

"I hear you." For what that was worth. "Talk to you later. Now I gotta run." He had pictures to collect. And a visit to the condo where he'd spent some of the most exciting and unforgettable nights of his life.

THIRTY MINUTES LATER, Durk pulled into the parking garage attached to Meghan's high-rise complex. He noted the cameras that monitored his movements and those of anyone else entering or leaving via the garage. He was fairly certain the film from yesterday was already in the hands of Detective Smart. Hopefully it held valuable clues as to the identity of the attacker Meghan had yet to recall.

Her memories were suppressed. Durk's were far too potent as he pressed the magnetic key into the door that opened into the first-floor hallway.

A midnight swim in the rooftop pool followed by hours of making love. Slow dancing on the moonlit private balcony to a country ballad with Meghan dressed only in a pair of red Western boots that he'd had made for her.

Reveries that he didn't need now.

He took the elevator to the fifth floor, an elevator that was also equipped with security cameras. Oddly, he remembered thinking how protected the condo was the first time he'd come here with Meghan.

It had given him an obviously false sense of Meghan's safety. Not that safety had been a major concern of hers. She'd frequently assured him she could take care of herself and that she was always packin'.

But where was her gun when the attacker showed up? He should have been the one who was shot and left to die in a pool of his own blood.

The elevator bell clanged, the door opened and Durk stepped out just as Bill Mackey was about to step in.

"Just the man I need to talk to," Durk said, putting out a hand to the muscular brute of a guy he'd mostly seen in passing. They'd engaged in exactly one actual conversation before this.

Bill shook his hand with a bodybuilder's grip as the elevator left without him. "Haven't run into you around here in years," Bill said. "I guess you must have heard what happened to Meghan last night."

"I did. In fact, I just left the hospital."

"How is she?"

"She has a concussion and has a nice little goose egg on her head, but she's going to be fine."

"Thank God. That son of a bitch would have killed her if I hadn't shown up when I did. I saw him bash her head against the wall."

"Did you get a good look at him?"

"No, but I got a piece of him. I would have finished the thug off if he hadn't got in one lucky punch."

"Tell me what you saw after you arrived on the scene."

"The guy had Meghan pinned to the wall with his body. He had his fist pulled back and was about to punch her in the face when I rushed in. I ordered the yellow-bellied woman-killer to get his hands off her and take on me."

"Then what happened?"

"He got one look at me and he was ready to run. He took hold of Meghan's shoulders and bashed her head against the wall. Then he turned and pointed a Taser at me."

"Did you see a pistol?"

"No. All he had was a Taser."

"Did he use that on you?"

"He would have. Before he could, Meghan kicked him and ruined his aim. I wrestled it from his hand and tossed it across the room."

"What was Meghan doing during this time?"

"When I saw her she was just lying on the floor. I think she was unconscious, probably from having her head bashed into the wall. But she'd still managed to get in that kick that kept him from Tasering me before she passed out. She's a fighter."

"She is that. Any chance you can identify the assailant?"

"No. I tried to yank off his mask, but that was when he got his one lucky punch below the belt.

I staggered backward and the punk coward took off like the devil himself was at his heels."

"Did you go after him?"

"No. I figured getting an ambulance for Meghan was more urgent."

"A good call," Durk agreed. "Did you see any identifying characteristics on the attacker? A tattoo? A scar? Any kind of prominent mole, birthmark or disfigurement?"

"No. Detective Smart already asked me all of that. About all I can tell you is that he was over six feet tall and muscular. And he's a white guy. That I can guarantee since I saw his fists up close and personal."

"I see the evidence," Durk said, eyeing a nasty bruise below Bill's right eye, proof that the guy had gotten in at least one punch far above the waist, too.

"I still don't understand how the guy got into the building," Bill said. "Management keeps stressing how secure the complex is when talking to prospective buyers."

"Where there's a will, there's a way," Durk said. It was a meaningless cliché. His mind had already moved on to other considerations, like why the man had used a stun gun on Meghan and tried to use one on Bill when he'd used a bullet on Ben Conroe.

Bill reached over and pressed the call button for the elevator. "Any idea when Meghan will be coming home?"

"The doctor hasn't said."

"Tell her I asked about her."

"Will do."

The elevator showed up and this time Bill did step inside it. There had been no mention of Ben's death. Evidently Bill had bypassed all the local news media that morning.

Questions about the vile perpetrator and why he'd targeted Meghan persisted as Durk stalked down the hallway toward Meghan's door. As expected, it was crisscrossed with police crime scene tape. Durk moved the tape, inserted his key and stepped inside.

His insides recoiled at the scene, obviously left pretty much as the cops had found it. An end table was overturned, its contents resting among shards of broken glass from a shattered vase. The lamp that had stood next to her sofa was overturned and broken.

Fingerprint powder dusted the surface of tabletops and the floor. A stringent odor he didn't recognize hung heavy in the air, no doubt some chemical used by the CSU in their quest for clues. Their search would have been much more intense than usually provided for an unarmed attack since it was connected to a murder, as well.

A sickening feeling churned in Durk's stomach when his gaze fell on the blood stains that darkened the wall next to the balcony door. He imagined the brutal bastard bashing Meghan's head into the wall. This time the wave of fury was so strong it made him nauseous.

There was no way Meghan could come home to this until after the police tape was removed and the place was cleaned up.

He forced himself to turn his back on the living room and stepped into Meghan's bedroom. The familiarity of it was painful, but he kept the memories at bay. They would get him nowhere and he didn't have time to waste reliving the past.

He studied a few framed photographs that rested on top of Meghan's chest. He chose two. One was of her and some of her sorority sisters when she'd attended Baylor. She'd told Durk all about them when they'd first started dating. He knew she was still close to all of them though none lived in the Dallas area.

The other picture was a professional shot of her and Lucy on Lucy's wedding day. Their arms were around each other's shoulders and they were laughing. A moment as meaningful as that surely couldn't have faded totally from Meghan's mind.

He walked over to the bedside table and picked up a silver-framed snapshot of Meghan, Lucy and their mother taken on the day Meghan had left for college. This was probably enough for a start, but he lingered a minute and then opened the drawer.

There were a couple of paperback novels, a flashlight and two packaged condoms. He felt an instant irritation that even he couldn't justify. He hadn't expected Meghan's sex life to end just because they'd broken up. But if there was a significant other in her life, where was he now?

He was about to slam the drawer shut when he spotted what appeared to be another picture, this one barely poking out from beneath the bottom book.

He fit his fingers around the corner and removed it from the drawer. The snapshot stared back at him mockingly. It was of him, asleep in her bed, his thick, dark hair mussed, his chest bared. He'd had no idea she'd taken it, even less idea why she'd kept it.

He added it to the collection, though he wasn't sure he should show it to her. It contradicted the story that they were just friends and might make her nervous to be around him.

He turned to go and was almost home free when he heard footsteps outside the door. Keys clanged and then one turned in the lock. For a second he thought it might be the assailant returning and he looked for a weapon, his body gearing up for a fight.

But when the door opened, it was Sam Smart's consternation he faced.

"Anyone ever tell you what the penalty is for ignoring Police Do Not Cross Tape?"

"Can't say that they have."

"Don't get smart, Lambert. Your being a Dallas big shot doesn't score you any points with me."

"I wouldn't expect it to. Any luck with tracking down Meghan's attacker?"

"Nothing I'm at liberty to discuss." Smart's mouth twisted into a scowl. "What are you doing here?"

"I just came by to pick up some snapshots that might help jog Meghan's memory," he answered truthfully. "No chance she can identify the man who sent her to the hospital unless she remembers him."

"So you're just trying to help me do my job." The detective stuck out his hand. "Let me see the pictures."

Durk wished he'd left the one of him sleeping

tucked away in the drawer, but there was nothing he could do now but turn it over with the rest of the pictures.

Smart sneered when he came to it. "I don't even want to think about what memories you're trying to revive with this one."

Durk swallowed the first comment that came to mind, figuring that pissing off Smart wouldn't help him get this over with any sooner. "You know, I'd really like to get back to the hospital with these as soon as I can," Durk said.

Smart handed him back the photos. "Okay, Lambert. You can walk—for now. But cross this line again and you go straight to jail. Is that clear?"

"Suppose Meghan wants something from here?" Durk asked. "It's still her home."

"If Meghan needs anything from the apartment before we remove the barrier tape, I'll get it for her," Smart said.

"Have it your way." Either Smart didn't like him on general principle or he thought Durk might not be totally innocent. For whatever reason, Smart was not going to make Durk's involvement in this easy.

No matter. Durk had no intention of backing out until someone was arrested and behind bars. He didn't plan for that to be him.

He took the pictures and left, thankful to get away from Smart and the memory-filled condo. Before he reached the hospital, his phone rang. This time it was his brother Tague.

"You need to get back to the hospital, Durk. And make it fast. You've got big problems on your hands."

Chapter Six

"What's wrong?" Durk fought the rising panic. "Is it Meghan? Are there complications?"

"The problem is not with Meghan," Tague assured him. "At least not yet."

"Then what is it?"

"I was approaching the telemetry unit nurses' station to see if I could find you when this woman showed up demanding to see Meghan."

Durk gave a low whistle. "Man, don't scare me like that. The woman's probably a friend of Meghan's who just read or heard about the attack."

"She's not sounding too friendly. She claims that Meghan killed her husband. I'd say she's definitely here to make trouble."

"Did you call security?"

"She was bordering on hysteria. I didn't have the heart to have her thrown out or possibly arrested."

"You surely didn't let her in to see Meghan?"

"No. I persuaded her to come down to the hospital coffee shop with me and talk things through."

"What's her story?"

"She claims she's Ben Conroe's wife."

Damn. Durk had been so upset about Meghan that he hadn't given any thought to Ben's wife. He should have broken the news of her husband's death to her instead of leaving it to the police. It might not have been nearly as cold coming from him.

"Is she there by herself?" Durk asked.

"Yeah. She told me her parents are driving over from Georgia, but they won't be here until tonight."

"She must have friends or a pastor she can call to help her through this."

"She's not too concerned about being here alone. All she wants to do is confront the woman she thinks is responsible for her husband's death."

"She can't go in and upset Meghan. That's out of the question. Besides, at this point, Meghan won't even know who she is."

"You'd better get back here and explain that to her. You know I'm allergic to hysterical women. They make me break out in hives."

"It's strawberries that do that."

"Then Mary Nell Conroe must be wearing strawberry-scented perfume."

DURK SPOTTED TAGUE, Mary Nell and his mother sitting together at a back table in the hospital coffee shop. He had no idea how Carolina had gotten dragged into the situation, but it was no doubt for the best.

No one was better at providing a little TLC and understanding—or at forcing a person to deal with facts head-on—if that's what she thought was needed.

Mary Nell's elbows were propped on the table and her hands were cradling her head. Durk quickly made his way to the table, pulled out a chair and joined them.

"This is my son Durk," Carolina said.

Mary Nell lifted her head and stared at him warily, as if he were a wolf joining their group of nervous sheep. Her eyes were red and swollen and her hay-colored hair looked as if someone had twisted it into knots before loosening it to fly wild.

"You're the one who found Ben's body," she accused, her stare reproachful.

"I went to Meghan's office to tell Ben that

Meghan was in the hospital," Durk said. "I never expected to find him dead."

"You wouldn't have gone there if you hadn't suspected something was wrong. Meghan told you he was in danger. Don't deny it. She probably sent you to warn him, but you didn't get there in time."

Durk worked to keep his voice calm. "You have this all wrong, Mary Nell. Meghan had no idea I was going to look for Ben. She'd been assaulted and needed emergency care to save her own life."

"It's still her fault. She should have realized the killer was on to her scheme."

Now they were getting somewhere. "What scheme is that?"

"Whatever scheme Meghan had going. She was always putting herself and Ben in danger."

Durk could all but hear the thud when they hit nowhere again. "Look, I'm really sorry about Ben, Mary Nell," Durk said, determined not to sound defensive. He'd done nothing that needed defending. "But his death was a criminal act. The only person to blame is the one who pulled the trigger."

Mary Nell pushed back from the table and jumped out of her chair. "Everybody always sides with Meghan, the same as Ben did. But

I'm tired of staying silent. I won't stop until I talk to every reporter in Dallas. And I'll tell Meghan Sinclair exactly how I feel to her face."

Not today she wasn't, not if Durk had to physically carry her out of the hospital and escort her home. "You have every right to be distressed, but I won't let you upset Meghan. Unless you have something to tell me about the case Meghan and Ben were working on, you need to go home and call a friend to come and stay with you."

"I'll tell you about the case. Ben was worried. I overheard him warn Meghan the night before to back off and let the police handle this one. She didn't listen. She never listens."

"What else did you hear him say?"

"I don't remember. Something about the situation getting out of hand and it being too risky."

Durk had no trouble believing that. Meghan would do anything to solve one of her cases, even dangle herself out there like a worm on a fishhook. He felt the old frustrations building.

"Try to remember if Ben said anything else about the case. It could help us find your husband's killer."

Mary Nell shuddered and sat back down. "I don't remember. But he was upset. He hardly slept that night after talking to Meghan."

Carolina put a hand over Mary Nell's. "I know

this is hard for you," Carolina said, "but you need to stay strong and focused. We want to help you, but you have to tell us what Meghan was doing that was so dangerous."

Tears filled Mary Nell's eyes and began to stream down her cheeks. Carolina handed her one of the paper napkins in lieu of a tissue.

"I've begged Ben time and again to quit his job. He was going to be a father. He shouldn't risk his life just because Meghan had a death wish."

"Are you expecting a baby?" Carolina asked.

Mary Nell placed her hands on her stomach. "I'm almost four months pregnant," she said through her tears and sobs. "Ben was so excited. Now he'll never see his child."

Carolina wrapped her arms around Mary Nell's shoulders.

Durk's heart went out to her, but he really needed Mary Nell to be coherent. "Did Ben mention a name? Please, think hard. Did he ever say the name of either the client who had hired him for this job or the person Meghan was tracking?"

"No."

"Did he ever say what made this person particularly dangerous?"

"No. He never told me names or any details

about his work, not until a case was closed. He claimed he wanted to protect me from the sordid situations he dealt in. He should have been protecting himself."

Mary Nell dabbed her eyes with the napkin.

"Did Ben have a home office?" Durk asked, still hoping for some clue that would lead to the killer.

"No. He usually just worked on his laptop at the kitchen table when he had something to do for the detective agency. What work he had that wasn't on the computer, he kept in his briefcase."

"Where are his computer and briefcase now?"

"I don't know. I would have thought they'd be at the office with Ben. Apparently they weren't since Detective Smart questioned me about them, too."

"When did you talk to him?"

"Last night, but I was so upset, I barely remember it. If I had Ben's computer or laptop, I would have given it to Detective Smart. Police should be the ones to track down criminals."

"But they sometimes fail," Tague said, finally breaking into the conversation. "They did with my wife, Alexis. That's why I hired Meghan to help us keep her safe from a killer. Meghan is very good at what she does. I'm sure Ben was, too."

"He was good at everything," Mary Nell said. "He was smart and kind and loving. And now he's dead. But it should be Meghan waiting to be buried. I'll tell her that. I swear I will."

There would be no reasoning with Mary Nell today, but she had said enough to convince Durk that this was connected to a current case. There had to be records of the investigation, and no doubt those were the records the man had been after when he'd shot and killed Ben. That would explain the files scattered all over the office floor.

Carolina's cell phone rang. She excused herself and took the call. When she returned she remained standing. "That was Sybil. The doctor has released her. Tague, why don't you drive her home? Alexis, Emma and Grandma Pearl are all at the ranch. They can help take care of Sybil until I get home."

"Where will you be?" Durk asked, though he could easily guess the answer.

"I'll drive Mary Nell home and stay with her until her parents arrive."

"I'm not leaving the hospital," Mary Nell declared through another round of sobs. "Not until I see Meghan."

"Then I'll stay with you while you wait to

see her," Carolina said calmly. "Durk, you and Tague can go now. Mary Nell and I will be fine."

Durk was hesitant to leave her, but he'd seen his mother in action too many times to doubt that she would get through to Mary Nell.

Carolina was a spiritual miracle worker. Even their pastor called her in when dealing with severely crushed spirits and broken hearts. Empathy was second nature to her.

Carolina sat down beside Mary Nell.

"I loved Ben so much," Mary Nell said between sobs. "I don't want to live without him."

"I know," Carolina said. "I understand completely. I lost my beloved husband, too, just over a year ago. But you have your baby to think of and part of Ben will live on through your child."

"Mom's amazing," Tague said as he and Durk walked away.

"You're right," Durk agreed. "I know she still grieves for Dad, but sometimes I forget how close they were."

"That's love," Tague said. "When it moves in, it claims your heart and soul."

"Then you guys can keep it. I like controlling my own destiny."

"You'll change your tune when you get struck by Cupid—unless…"

Durk knew exactly where Tague was going

with that. "Meghan Sinclair is just a friend," he said, attempting to set the record straight.

"Keep telling yourself that, bro."

He planned to. At some point he might even start believing it.

"I guess I better go get Aunt Sybil," Tague said. "If I don't, she'll send someone to find me."

"Right. Thanks for coming in and for the timely arrival."

"You bet," Tague said. "I'll see you at the ranch whenever you get there or before if you need me."

But what Durk needed right now was a name, and that was locked away somewhere in Meghan's trauma-fogged memory. Hopefully the snapshots would be the key to unlocking it.

When he reached Meghan's room, she was sound asleep. The nurse on the day shift sent him away, claiming that Meghan needed her rest.

He killed the next hour going back to the penthouse to pick up his laptop and going over everything he'd heard over the last twelve hours. He tried to imagine the train of events that had led to the attack and the murder.

Meghan was as daring and as indomitable as Mary Nell had said. He knew that as well as anybody. In most instances, it had paid off, but somehow she'd screwed up this time and allowed the killer to get the upper hand.

But why go after her with a stun gun and then go after Ben with a loaded pistol? The fact that he'd worn a mask would indicate that he'd never intended to kill her. Was the attack meant to be a threat?

But if the man had actually planned to kill her, what was to stop him from trying again?

MEGHAN WOKE SLOWLY, pushed through the lingering miasma and looked around. The first thing she saw was the cowboy sitting near her bed, working on his laptop. Reality gained a foothold.

"You're back," she murmured.

"Yes. I've been here for over an hour."

"Why didn't you wake me?"

"I was given an ultimatum by Patricia, the fire-breathing day nurse. Disturb you and I'm out of here."

"I've slept enough," Meghan said. "I need to stop floating in the clouds and become grounded."

And to do that, she needed Durk. He was her only real bond with herself, the only person she'd communicated with since regaining consciousness who actually knew Meghan Sinclair.

"Can I get you anything?" Durk asked.

"A sip of water. My throat and my lips feel parched."

He stood and walked around the bed to get the water, but before he got the straw to her lips, the nurse came in and took over the task.

"How are you feeling?" she asked as she returned the glass to the bed tray.

"Stiff. Sore. And tired of this bed."

Patricia raised the head of her bed so that Meghan was in a sitting position. "The doctor left orders that you can take a short walk if you feel like it."

"That would be great."

"The key word is *short*," Patricia said. "Just a few doors down the hall and back again. But you'll need someone with you to steady you if you get dizzy."

"I can take care of that," Durk offered.

"Okay, but take it slow with her. I don't want my patient to exert herself too much." She leaned over and fluffed Meghan's pillows. "Is there anything else I can do for you?"

"Can you tell me when I'll be released from the hospital?"

"That, I have no control over."

"But she has control over everything else that

happens in this room," Meghan said once Patricia was out of earshot.

"You must be getting better. I sense a power struggle here."

"I have a feeling that when I'm not lost in la-la land, I must like being the one in control."

Durk smiled. "I'd say that's a fair assessment."

He looked incredibly handsome when he smiled. It was hard to imagine she could have let him slip from her memory no matter how severe the concussion.

"Tell me about me, Durk. Not what I did for a living. Patricia's already told me that I'm a private investigator with my own agency. She also filled me in on my parents. My parents are dead. I have a sister named Lucy. She's married and lives in Connecticut. She wants me to call her as soon as I feel like talking."

"Where did your nurse get all of that information?"

"Apparently Lucy has called several times today to check on me. She and Patricia have pretty much shared my life history. Patricia can't understand why I refuse to talk to Lucy when she calls."

"Why do you?"

"I'm just not ready."

"Talking to her might help shake the amnesia," Durk suggested.

"Which makes the prospect sound tempting, but no. Not yet." This was frustrating enough without bringing a family member into the mix, someone with whom she'd shared a lifetime of vanished memories.

"Tell me some personal things about myself, Durk."

"I thought you wanted to go for a walk."

"That can wait a few minutes."

"What kind of personal things would you like to know? That you like country music and have every recording George Strait ever made on your iPod? That you live with a phone in your hand? That you have a serious crush on Hugh Jackman?"

"Hugh Jackman." She pictured him in her mind without any trouble. "*The Boy from Oz.* Wolverine. And who could forget him with Nicole Kidman in *Australia?*"

Durk's eyebrows arched. "You remember Hugh Jackman but not your sister?"

"Evidently. Odd, isn't it?"

"Maybe not so odd," Durk said. "Your memory may be starting with the impersonal."

"That makes it even more frustrating. I remember movies and plays, but not my friends and family. I remember songs, but not where I live. I remember that Christmas is on December 25, but I can't tell you where I spent any Christmas in my life. And I don't remember you."

"Perhaps I'm not that memorable."

She seriously doubted that. "Did I meet you through my business? Were you a philandering husband that I spied on for a jealous wife?"

"I've never had a wife."

"Then how did we meet?"

"I attended a charity fundraiser where you were working a case and pretending to be someone you weren't."

"Since when do cowboys attend charity fundraisers?"

"It's a long story."

"I'll bet."

Durk raked his fingers through his hair and leaned in closer. "What else do you want to know?"

"What kind of person am I? Sweet and loving or bossy and demanding?"

Durk laughed out loud. "*Sweet* is definitely not the first word that comes to mind when I think about you."

"What is?"

"Vivacious. Feisty. Professional. Sexy."

"Are you sure you don't have me mixed up with someone else?"

"I'm certain."

"I don't feel any of those things today, and I sure don't look the part."

"You will again. And it won't take you long. You're a take-charge kind of gal."

"What's the worst thing you can say about me? Tell me the truth. I promise I won't get mad."

"You break promises," he teased. "And you take too many risks in your work."

He didn't sound like he was teasing with the risk accusation, but Meghan didn't necessarily see that as a negative. "Am I good at what I do?"

"Exceptionally good."

"Then maybe the risks are worth it."

"You're usually convinced that they are."

From his tone, she'd guess he didn't agree. "Do you think those risks led to my being attacked?"

"I think it's highly likely."

But no one would know for certain until she could remember the man who'd assaulted her. That made regaining her memory all the more critical.

"How old am I, Durk?"

"Thirty-one. Your birthday was in August."

"Thirty-one and still single."

"That's by design. You could have your choice of any number of men."

She wondered if he was one of them. "Are you married or engaged?"

"No," he answered quickly. "Also by design."

"So we're both single but our relationship is strictly platonic? You must not find me attractive."

"There's not a man alive who doesn't find you attractive. We dated a few times a couple of years ago, but it didn't work out."

"Did I break it off or did you?"

He looked down and fidgeted with one of the handles on her bed.

"I'm sorry, Durk. I didn't mean to make you uncomfortable. I'm just trying to get a feel for who I am."

"I'm not uncomfortable, Meghan. And there's no reason not to tell you the truth. We were lovers, but we both realized early on that a long-term relationship wouldn't work. You were actually the one who sent me packing."

They hadn't worked out, but he was here with her now and couldn't be more attentive. She was comfortable with him and found him incredibly attractive.

Would that change when her memory returned? Was there a side of him she wouldn't like? Or was there a side of her that pushed men away?

"I stopped by your condo this morning and picked up a few snapshots that might stir your memory," Durk said. "Would you like to look at them?"

"Sure. Do you have one of me without knots and bruises?"

"I do." He took a five-by-seven photograph from a folder he retrieved from his laptop case and placed it in her hands. "This is you and your sister the day she got married."

Meghan studied the images and held her breath, waiting for an epiphany. None came. She continued to study the print.

Her sister was several inches shorter than her, especially since Meghan was wearing nosebleed stilettos. Lucy was stunning with beautiful eyes and a killer body.

"My sister is gorgeous."

"You both are," Durk corrected.

"But I'm not stunning the way she is."

"No, you have your own style and assets. You're a natural beauty. No need for makeup and you don't usually wear much."

His words weren't borne out by the photo. "Tall and skinny are not really assets."

"No, but tall and willowy, with a tantalizing spray of freckles over the bridge of your perfect nose are. Not to mention your shiny auburn hair that falls around your shoulders in cascades of soft curls. Or the fact that you wear a perfume of self-confidence. That's extremely seductive, you know."

"Yes, and now my shiny hair will be accentuated by bald spots." She dropped the photograph on the top of the lightweight blanket. "Let's see the next picture."

Durk handed her another snapshot, this one in black-and-white. "This one is of you and some of your sorority sisters from your days at Baylor. That's you in the middle."

There were five young women in all. They looked incredibly young and delightfully carefree. And she was right there in the center of the fun. She couldn't remember ever having seen a single one of them before.

Her frustration swelled. "This is probably a waste of time."

"Try one more," Durk urged. He took the photograph from her and pressed the next one into her hands.

This time it was her and— A sharp flash of pain made her suck in her breath as she studied the second person in the picture. Her mind drew a blank, but her emotions had reacted. "Is this my mother?"

"It is. It was taken a short time before her death. You winced when you saw it. It must have struck a chord."

"It struck a chord with my emotions. My mind is still drawing a blank."

Disappointment dragged her down to a new low. She knew she needed to stay calm and optimistic, but how could she when her world had skidded out of control and she couldn't get it back?

All because someone had brutally attacked her in her own home. Had it not been for a neighbor she couldn't even remember, she'd likely be dead.

Had she known the man who did this to her? Was he someone she'd been tracking or spying on as part of her job? Was she so afraid of him that a part of her mind had shut down rather than face him?

And where was he now? For all she knew he could be in this very hospital, watching and waiting to finish what he'd started. Her own brain had become the traitor that could cost her life.

Icy tingles of terror shimmied up her spine.

"Let's go for that walk, Durk." Before she succumbed to fear of what she couldn't remember or even begin to understand.

BY THE TIME DR. LEVY arrived for his rounds, Meghan was more frustrated than ever. Physically, she felt fine. She'd even made progress in her mental status. She could answer impersonal questions without any trouble. She knew who the president was. She knew who'd penned "The Star-Spangled Banner." She even knew that Austin was the capital of Texas.

She remembered everything that had happened since Dr. Levy had visited with her and Durk in the wee hours of the morning.

But she had zero memory of anything personal that had happened before this morning.

Dr. Levy examined her chart. "Everything looks good," he said. "Your vital signs are stable. There's been no new bleeding from the wounds we stapled. The nurse says you're getting around on your own without any trouble. And there's been no dizziness or nausea since this morning."

Which left the real dilemma unspoken. "So why hasn't my memory returned?"

"Sometimes that takes a little more time."

"How long can retrograde amnesia last?"

"That depends on a number of factors. With the type of concussion you had, distant memories are usually recovered in hours or days. The events immediately preceding the concussion can sometimes take months to recover. It can be even longer if there are underlying emotional factors."

"Can't you give me something to speed up the recovery process?"

"I'm afraid there are no drugs for that, nor would I prescribe them if there were. Drugs would be far more likely to interfere with regaining your mental status and make your progress more difficult to assess."

"So all I can do is sit around and wait for the memories to kick in."

"That's basically it for now. If we don't see any progress with the long-term memory within a few days, we can bring in a psychiatrist to evaluate whether the extant emotional factors are playing a part in the amnesia."

"Or maybe I can just send out an SOS for my attacker to come back again and give me a second chance to identify him." She stood and paced the small room. "I'm sorry. I didn't mean to sound ungrateful. I'm just so bewildered and frustrated with all of this."

"I understand," Dr Levy said. "But it's too early for any kind of SOS yet. You have to give this some time."

"Maybe getting out of the hospital and back to my normal surroundings would help."

Dr. Levy nodded. "That's an option."

"Not in this case," Durk said. "Your condo is still decorated with police tape and fingerprint dust. It will need a thorough cleaning before it's livable again."

"That eliminates that possibility," Dr. Levy agreed. "Do you have a friend you can stay with?"

She shrugged. "How would I know?"

"You can stay with me in my condo," Durk offered.

Sure, if living with temptation and a past lover was the answer to her problems. "That might be a little too cozy."

"We could stay on the ranch," he said. "There's plenty of room and lots of chaperones if that's what you're worried about."

"Chaperones?"

"My family. My mother, my aunt, my grand-mother, two brothers and their wives and children."

She shook her head. "I don't think I'm ready to face that many strangers."

Durk leaned against the end of her bed. "Right now everyone in the world is a stranger to you,

Meghan. At the ranch, at least I'd know you were safe."

"You will need someone around to watch out for you until your memory improves," Dr. Levy said. "But we don't have to make that decision tonight. I'd like you to stay in the hospital at least one more night. In the morning, I'll either release you or move you out of the telemetry unit and into a regular private room."

"I can go along with that," she agreed.

"Good. Now we can move to the next issue. Detective Sam Smart from the Dallas Police Department has been waiting since last night to talk to you."

"Did you tell him I can't remember the attack?"

"I did, but he still wants to talk to you. I've put him off as long as I can."

"Then send him in. In fact, I'd like to know more about the attack and where he stands in the investigation. If nothing else, he should have fingerprints."

"Before she sees the detective, I'm going to need a minute alone with her," Durk said.

The doctor nodded. "I thought you might. I'll have the detective wait ten minutes before coming in. When he does, he'd like to see Meghan alone."

That, Meghan didn't like. "I'd prefer Durk stay with me."

"The nurse will be right outside. You can ring her if there's a problem or an emergency," the doctor said.

"That won't stop the detective from trying to intimidate her," Durk protested. "If he starts harassing her, couldn't that upset her enough to impede her recovery?"

"That's a possibility. I can't keep him from seeing you alone forever, but I can medically justify you not being questioned without someone you trust in the room for one more night." The doctor lowered the chart and stepped closer to the bed. "Your call, Meghan."

"I prefer Durk be here," she said without hesitation.

There was no reason for her to dread being alone with the detective, but the thought of it set her nerves on edge.

"Then you can stay, Durk. And, Meghan, if the questioning becomes too stressful, ring for the nurse."

Patricia sported a genuine smile. "Yes, and give me the pleasure of kicking him out. The man's been bugging me all day."

Dr. Levy made a few notes on her chart and left with the nurse at his heels.

She finger combed her hair, took a sip of water and turned back to Durk. "You're down to nine minutes. What is it you wanted to tell me before the detective arrives?"

He squirmed and repositioned himself in his chair. "Does the name Ben Conroe sound familiar to you?"

"Ben." She let the name roll off her tongue. "Ben Conroe."

The name was vaguely familiar. That had to be a good sign. Perhaps she was on the verge of a memory breakthrough.

But when she looked at Durk, she was overcome with a pervasive fear that the worst was yet to come.

Chapter Seven

"Who is Ben Conroe?" Meghan asked, suddenly anxious to get this new revelation out in the open.

"He was your assistant."

"Was?"

"Ben was murdered last night in your office, around the same time that you were attacked."

She wrapped her fingers around the rungs of the bed rail, clutching them so tightly that pain shot up her arms. The nausea hit in waves, but this time she doubted it was related to the concussion.

Fighting back burning tears, she met Durk's gaze. "Is this ever going to end?"

"Not until we know who's behind the violence."

She tried to make sense of the sickening circumstances. "The attack and the murder must be connected, probably carried out by the same depraved person."

"I'm sure they're connected, but unless the detective has evidence to the contrary, we can't be certain how many perpetrators were involved."

"But it's entirely possible that the killer left my condo and went directly to my office, where he encountered and killed my employee," she said.

"I'd say there's a damn good chance it happened exactly like that," Durk agreed.

"Ben Conroe." Meghan repeated his name several times, as if the repetition would force memories of him to explode in her mind. When they didn't, her spirits sank to rock bottom. "This is so frustrating. I feel a sickening sense of loss, as if I'm grieving for a friend. Yet I can't remember him at all."

"Maybe your mind is protecting you until your body has recovered enough to handle his death."

"I don't want to be protected, at least not like that." Impulsively, she touched her fingertips to the swollen knot behind her temple and then to the bandages that covered her wounds. The man who did this to her was a killer. It was a miracle she was alive. Ben hadn't been granted a miracle.

"How old was Ben?"

"I'm not sure," Durk said. "In his late twenties, I'd guess."

"Did you know him well?"

"No. I met him a couple of times when you and I were dating. We'd talk a few minutes when I picked you up at the office. That was the extent of it. But I know the two of you worked closely together and you spoke very highly of him."

"Was he married?"

"Yes. His wife's name is Mary Nell."

And now she was a widow. "Do they have children?"

He hesitated and looked away—never a good sign. "Don't even think about lying to protect me, Durk. I don't want twisted half-truths that will only confuse me more."

"Mary Nell is four months pregnant."

"Oh, no. How horribly sad." But something seemed odd. "How do you know so much about Ben's wife?"

"She showed up at the hospital this morning. I talked to her briefly."

"She was here? Why didn't someone tell me?"

"You were resting. And you're supposed to be staying calm. If just talking about Ben's death is hitting you this hard, imagine how difficult talking to his widow would be."

"Stay calm? In the midst of this terror and chaos? You might as well tell me to gaze into a crystal ball and conjure up the name of the killer." She kicked the blanket off her legs. Not that she was hot. She just needed to kick something.

"I should at least call Ben's wife."

"I wouldn't," Durk said. "Not yet."

"She came to see me. She must want to talk."

"You'll just upset both of you if you try to talk about Ben's death while you can't even remember him. You should wait."

"I'll think about it."

Durk leaned over the bed and rubbed her bruised arm, gingerly, as if he were comforting a small child or an aging aunt. But he was staring out the window and his mind was clearly grappling with more than whether she called Mary Nell now or later.

"Why do I think there's more you're not telling me?" she asked.

"Because you're one of the most perceptive P.I.s in the business."

"Then spill it."

"I may as well. If I don't, Detective Smart will. I'm the one who went to your office and found Ben's body, Meghan."

Confusion settled in again. "You found the

body? How did that happen? You said you only ran into me at the hospital while you were checking on your aunt."

"I did, but since I was the only person around who knew you, I was enlisted to provide pertinent information—like your name, age, address. But that was basically all I could give them."

Meghan listened to Durk's account of how he went to her office for information and found Ben's body instead. Worrisome doubts crept into her mind when he came to the part about why his fingerprints were all over the pistol left near Ben's body.

All she really knew of Durk Lambert was what he had told her. She had no way of knowing if any of it was true. He could be a conniving imposter.

He admitted that he hadn't seen her in two years before last night. He claimed that they were once lovers but that it hadn't worked out. He explained that running into her last night was purely coincidental.

And yet he was the first person she'd seen when she woke up in this room and he'd barely left her side since. She reached over and let her fingers trace the smooth lines of his hands. Not the rough skin of a man who worked with animals and ropes and saddles, but a rich man's hands with clean nails and smooth knuckles. And the watch on his wrist was a Rolex.

Her instincts urged her to trust him. But why trust her instincts when her mental status was shaky at best?

She moved her hand away from his. A dozen questions plagued her mind. Before she could ask the first one, Detective Smart stepped inside the room and closed the door behind him.

He set a green canvas messenger bag on the seat of an empty chair. Then he crossed the room, glared at Durk and introduced himself to Meghan. "I'm sorry to disturb your recovery," Smart said as he flashed his ID, "but I know you want the person who did this to you apprehended as badly as I do."

"Believe me, I don't mind being questioned, but I don't see how I can be much help."

The detective slipped out of his navy-colored, slightly wrinkled sport coat. "Hope you don't mind. Seems a little hot in here to me."

"No, make yourself comfortable."

He draped the coat over the back of the chair that held his canvas tote. "Dr. Levy said the attack left you with a concussion and that it was causing some memory problems."

"Not just *some* memory problems," Durk corrected. "She's experiencing retrograde amnesia."

Smart nodded and propped his foot on the rung of a chair while he held on to the back of it. Meghan had the feeling he was trying too hard to be nonchalant.

"From the little I understand about retrograde amnesia, it seems it's an unpredictable condition. The memory loss can be spotty. Remember your name, but not your address. Remember the last time you went dancing, but not what you had for dinner last night. That type of thing."

"That hasn't been my experience to this point," Meghan assured him. "My loss is far more pervasive than that."

"If she says she doesn't remember, she doesn't remember," Durk said. "Pressuring her won't help, and I'm certain Dr. Levy told you that."

"I'm not pressuring, Lambert. Meghan and I are just talking."

The tension between the two men crackled like water on a hot skillet. She wondered if Smart actually considered Durk a suspect or if this was more of a macho power struggle between the two men. At any rate, she didn't feel pressured by Smart. But he was definitely trying to manipulate her.

She decided to get everything out in the open. "I don't remember anything about the attack or what happened prior to the attack. But Durk just told me about Ben Conroe. I'd think you'd be better off spending your time investigating the murder."

"I'm investigating every angle of both," Smart said. "Did Durk mention that his fingerprints are all over the murder weapon?"

"I explained to Meghan how that happened," Durk said, "the same as I explained it to you."

"I'm sure she agreed it was a good story."

"Has it been verified that the pistol in question is in fact the murder weapon?" Meghan asked.

"Now you sound like a private investigator," Smart said. "Either that or a defense attorney, almost like you're working for Durk."

She locked her gaze with Smart's. "You didn't answer my question."

He dropped his hands from the back of the chair and stepped closer to the bed. "We don't have a conclusive ballistics report as yet, but the bullet that killed Ben Conroe did come from the same caliber pistol as the one found at the crime scene."

"Do you know who the gun was registered to?"

"We do. The gun was registered to you, Meghan."

She tried to stay cool, but she winced at the news.

"The killer must have taken it from Meghan

when she tried to defend herself with it," Durk said. "Then he took it with him to her office and used it to kill Ben."

Her gun was used to kill Ben Conroe. Things were getting worse by the second. "My contribution to Ben's murder," Meghan lamented.

"Don't start blaming yourself for any of this," Durk said.

"At least not until we know what really went down," Smart added.

"Not ever," Durk insisted. "Meghan's the victim, not the villain. And for the record, I'm not the villain, either."

"I'm aware of the facts in the case, Lambert."

Everyone seemed to have a handle on the facts except her. "Did your investigation of the crime scene uncover any useful evidence other than the weapon?"

"I'm not at liberty to discuss evidential findings with you at this point," Smart said. He walked to the window, looked out for a second and then turned and leaned his tall frame against the sill. "What I need from you is a description of your attacker."

"And you know I can't give you that as long as the amnesia is blocking out my memory of that night."

"Then perhaps this will jog your memory,"

Smart said. "On the day you were attacked, a phone call was made to your office."

"I can't even remember where I live. How do you think I could possibly remember a phone call?"

"I doubt you ever heard this call, but you may recognize the voice."

"Do you have the recording with you?" Durk asked.

"Yes, I do."

Smart pulled the answering machine from the messenger bag and plugged it in. In seconds, a deep, smooth, downright seductive male voice filled the room. His words chilled Meghan to the bone.

"I can't wait to meet you in person, Meghan. I'm captivated by your picture and enchanted by your sexy Texas drawl. I do hope you're not just leading me on. I think I'm already falling in love with you. The hours will drag by until when we finally meet."

Her stomach lurched. "I set up a date with a killer."

"Possibly," Smart said. "We don't know for certain that the call and the crime are related. But it wouldn't be the first time you've insinuated yourself as bait to catch a criminal," the detective said, his tone coldly accusing.

"Meghan's a private investigator," Durk reminded him. "She does her job, just like you do."

Smart ignored him. "I'll leave you my card, Meghan. Call me on my cell phone immediately if you remember anything about the man who left the message or who attacked you. The longer this man goes free, the farther he may get from Dallas."

A man she'd likely lured into Ben's life as well as her own. Now Ben was dead. The guilt was suddenly crushing.

Detective Smart didn't back off. "No games this time, Meghan. I expect your full cooperation. If I find that you know something you're not sharing with me or that your amnesia is only a ruse, I promise I will prosecute you for interfering with a police investigation."

His intimidation attempt was over the top. "I was attacked. My associate was murdered. Why would you think I would lie to you?"

"Past history, Meghan."

Durk stood and walked over to the door. "You've said enough, Detective. I think it's time you take the answering machine and your threats and bullying and concentrate on finding Ben's killer."

"I'm going," Smart said. "But I'll be back tomorrow and the next day and the next day—

until either the perp is behind bars or Meghan regains her memory."

Smart unplugged his machine and repacked it. "Nothing personal, Meghan. I'm just doing my job."

Right, nothing personal except her past history, a history she couldn't remember.

The door closed behind Smart. Meghan took his card, looked at it for a second and then tossed it on the table next to her bed. "I certainly hope that wasn't the good cop."

"Smart's just trying to intimidate you."

"He's good at it. I don't think he cares much for either of us."

"The feeling is mutual, at least on my part."

"Same here, but I must have quite a reputation as a smart and talented P.I. if Smart thinks I could fake the amnesia."

"I don't think anyone who knows you would doubt that."

She stared Durk down. "Don't tell me you think I'm faking."

"I didn't say that. But I do think you're capable of pulling it off if you wanted to."

"Because of my past history?"

"Partly."

"You're absolutely right. If I were faking, Durk Lambert, I wouldn't admit it." She might as well keep the cowboy on his toes. "I wonder if the killer is still in the Dallas area," she said, changing the subject.

"He probably skipped town quick if he thinks you can identify him or if he's the one who left the message on your office phone."

"Now that I think about that, why would anyone be stupid enough to leave a message like that if they were planning to attack me? It sounds more like someone was being set up."

"That's a definite possibility," Durk agreed. "It would be nice if we had a motive for that."

"Do you know if I have security cameras either inside or outside my office or condo?"

"You definitely have them at your condo complex," Durk said. "I didn't notice any at your office, but that doesn't mean they're not there."

"I'm sure Smart has checked it out," she said. "He didn't mention my computer or cell phone, though. I wonder if my attacker made off with them."

"It seems unlikely since your neighbor indicated the attacker made a hurried exit. You have Smart's phone number. Give him a call."

"I have a better idea. I should pay a visit to my condo. If anything is going to jog my memory about the attack, the scene of the crime should."

"Now you sound like the pre-attack Meghan."

"Then why the scowl? Wouldn't that be a good thing?"

"Not necessarily in this situation. Not if you like staying alive."

"I do." But she had a strong suspicion that while ignorance might be bliss, knowledge and knowing whom to trust were the secrets of survival.

She didn't dare trust anyone yet. So when she left the hospital tomorrow morning, she'd be flying solo. Unfortunately, she had no safe place to land.

Chapter Eight

The hospital halls were deserted this time of night, though he could hear voices coming from the nurses' station a few yards in front of him. Hopefully he wouldn't have to pass it.

He slowed his pace to check the name on the door he was passing. The last name was Everett. He kept walking.

Head up. Shoulders straight. An easy, confident swagger, he reminded himself as he pushed up the sleeves of the freshly laundered lab coat. Swiping it from the locked supply room had been surprisingly easy, thanks to the small metal tool he'd purchased from a locksmith company.

No wonder there were so many break-ins in his neighborhood. Locks were a joke. Car locks. Condo locks. Nothing to it.

His pulse hiked and his hands grew clammy when he spotted a nurse walking toward him.

Stay cool. He managed a smile when she stopped in front of him.

"Can I help you?" she asked.

"Sure. I'm still finding my way around this wing. I'm Tom Farmer, one of the residents recently assigned to the Trauma Unit. Dr. Levy sent me up to update Meghan Sinclair's chart."

"I bet he's getting ready to move her to a new floor. I told him we'd likely need that bed for a new trauma patient by morning."

It was amazing how helpful a hospital's staff could be, especially if you approached them right. "You're right," he said. "Meghan will be gone soon." The irony pleased him.

"Her full chart is at the nurses' station. But the one the doctor probably wants updated is in the holder at the foot of her bed."

"Which room is that?"

"It's 305, just down the hall."

"I'll try not to wake her."

"I doubt she's asleep. I don't think her boyfriend has gone home yet."

Damn. Not what he needed. "I can't believe she has company this late. It's almost midnight. Don't you follow visitor's hours in this unit?"

"It all depends on the patient and the doctor. Meghan Sinclair is experiencing a serious form of retrograde amnesia following a concussion.

Dr. Levy thinks that having someone she knows stay with her might speed up the memory recovery process."

"Does she have company around the clock?"

"She did last night, but that was just after she was admitted. I expect her visitor to go home tonight, but I'm not her nurse. Angela Drake is. She probably knows more about what's going on."

"Thanks." He started to walk away.

The nurse continued to block his path. "I'm surprised Dr. Levy didn't call and let us know he was planning to move Meghan out of this unit. He usually does."

"It's been crazy in the E.R. tonight. He'll probably call when he finds time. Meghan's case sounds interesting," he said, changing the subject.

"It's the worst case of memory loss stemming from a concussion that I've ever seen," the nurse admitted. "Meghan doesn't remember anything prior to regaining consciousness in the hospital."

"So she has no idea who attacked her?"

"Not a clue. The doctor did finally let a detective from the DPD in to see her this afternoon, but she couldn't have told him anything useful."

"But it's just a temporary memory loss, right?"

"Right. It should run its course soon, unless there are emotional factors involved. But if you have to be out of it, you can't beat having Durk Lambert around to hold your hand."

"Durk Lambert as in Lambert Inc.?"

"Yes. He's been with her almost constantly. We're all envious of Angela for getting to see so much of him."

He couldn't care less about Durk Lambert, but having another person in the room would make finishing the job much more difficult. All he needed was a few minutes alone with Meghan. Suffocation was easy, quick and silent.

It was his method of choice, though this would be the first time he'd killed a woman in a hospital.

The shame was he couldn't kill her torturously slow so that he could get his kicks. Now it would be a pillow over the face until her lungs gave up the struggle for oxygen.

It was sad that it had to end this way for such a beautiful woman. But she had brought it all on herself.

Now he just had to find a place he could hang around unseen until the boyfriend went home. It would be a glorious ending to the chapter.

The book would go on. The setting would change to another town, perhaps even another state. He would miss Texas.

Chapter Nine

A frigid mist was falling. The icy crystals clung to Meghan's skin, stinging like a thousand bumblebees. She pulled the light jacket tighter. It was almost dark. She should be home by now, locked safely inside.

She searched for her house, but even the street no longer looked familiar. The houses had bolted doors and dark windows. They had yards, but no grass—only weeds and flowers that had turned a rusty brown. She was lost. She had to get back to her own street.

She tried to run, but the roots of a spiny tree reached out to trip her. Her feet entangled in the spiky clumps and she fell face-first into the mud.

Laughter filled the night, but when she looked up, she saw nothing. The people who mocked her were hiding behind the dark windows. They were safe. She was the only one left out in the cold.

Wind gusted through the trees with such force that she had to grab on to the trunk of a towering tree to keep from being blown backward. Thunder rumbled. She had to find her way home before it was too late.

Too late. Too late. Too late.

The words echoed all around her until they drowned out the sounds of the wind and her feet slapping against the pavement. She turned a corner. Now there were no houses. No shelter. No place where she would be safe.

Her legs ached. Her lungs burned. Her fate was sealed. She would never get home again. Her knees gave way and she crumbled to the dry, hard earth.

The ground beneath her began to rumble, and the sound of pounding hooves grew so loud it threatened to split her skull into jagged fragments.

A herd of wild horses stampeded toward her, all riderless except for one. The faceless rider reached out his hand as he went flying by. Their fingers brushed, but she couldn't catch hold. The horse and rider galloped away, leaving her alone in the dark.

Except that she wasn't alone. Someone was nearby, lurking in the shadows. She could hear his breathing and smell the sickly sweet fragrance of his aftershave.

There were no trees now. No houses. No horse.

She put her hand on her chest. Her gown was wet with cold sweat. Slowly, the room came into focus. She was in the hospital.

Thunder rolled in the distance and rain splattered the window panes. It was storming outside. No wonder the room was so much darker than usual. The only illumination was the rectangle of light that crept in from beneath the door.

Slowly, her pupils adjusted enough that she could see that Durk's chair was empty. He'd gone home. The nightmare had vanished, but she couldn't shake the eerie feeling that someone was standing nearby.

"Durk. Durk, are you in here?"

No one answered. Yet she was sure now that she could hear breathing. "Who's there?" She reached over to push the call button for the nurse. A hand closed over hers.

"Don't be afraid, Meghan. I'm only here to help."

Panic struck like lightning. She shoved the man backward, then skirted the rail on the opposite side of the bed and hit the floor feetfirst.

The door to her room flew open before she

could escape and she saw the man rush through it, the white of his clothes catching the light.

Oh, no. Had she been so entangled in the nightmare that she'd just attacked a nurse or maybe even a doctor?

She reached over, flicked on the lamp over her bed and then leaned against the wall. Her breath came in hard, fast gasps, and even now she wasn't sure if she was awake or still trapped in the nightmare.

The door opened again, but this time it was Durk who stepped inside. She'd never been happier to see anyone in her life.

"Meghan, what's wrong? You're white as a ghost."

"I had a nightmare."

He rushed to her, dropped the duffel he was carrying to the chair and took both her hands in his. "You're shaking and your gown is soaking wet. Let me help you back into bed."

"Not yet." She fought to shake off the hangover-like confusion that clouded her reasoning.

"Did you dream about the attack?" Durk asked.

"No. That would have been good. At least I might have gained some insight from that. The nightmare was just a terrifying mishmash like my life's become."

"You don't have to talk about it."

But she did because she was still having difficulty differentiating between subconscious images and reality. "I thought I had woken up. I was back in the hospital, but there was a man lurking in the dark shadows inside my room."

He put his arms around her and held her close. His touch was familiar and strange at the same time. Part of her wanted to pull away. But the urge to cling to him was too strong to resist.

"It was just a nightmare," Durk said. "I shouldn't have left you alone."

The door creaked open again. Meghan stepped out of Durk's embrace as Angela walked over and turned off the call button. Her eyes went from Meghan to the bed.

"It looks like you tangled with a herd of mad bedbugs," Angela said.

Meghan stared at the mussed linens. One corner of the fitted sheet had pulled completely loose and the blanket was in a wad. One pillow was on the floor a few feet from the bed as if she'd hurled it at the departing intruder who she still wasn't sure was real or phantom.

"She had a nightmare," Durk answered when Meghan didn't.

Angela poured some cool water from the bedside pitcher and handed the glass to Meghan.

"Must be all those repressed memories fighting their way out," Angela said. "Don't quote me on that. That was purely layman's conjecture."

A streak of lightning lit the room followed by a booming crash of thunder and a sudden dimming of the lights.

"The storm's intensifying," Angela said. "But don't worry, we have generator backup for all essential needs in case of a power outage."

Wind whistled around the building, adding a ghostly wail to the thunder and the sound of rain pelting against the glass. Perfect sound effects for a horrifying nightmare.

Now, with the lights on and Angela and Durk nearby, Meghan was beginning to doubt that the man in her room had been any more real than the one on the galloping horse. But just to be on the safe side…

"Was there a male staff member in my room a few minutes ago?" Meghan asked, trying to clarify the mystery.

"Not that I know of," Angela said. "Why do you ask?"

"Either I dreamed there was a man in my room or there actually was one in here."

"There are two male nurses on duty tonight. We tend to look in on each other's patients when it's storming. Or one of them might have heard you call out during the nightmare and looked in to make sure you were all right."

"If there was one in here, apologize to him for my shoving him away. I was still in the throes of the nightmare."

Angela frowned. "In that case you must have been dreaming. Neither Cary nor Jim would have been scared off by you. And if they'd thought they'd upset you, they would have come and told me."

"Then chalk it up to the nightmare."

The man had seemed real. But then so had the man on the horse and she knew a horse hadn't galloped through her room. Meghan finished her water, set the glass on the tray and began to straighten her bed.

"Don't bother with that. I'll send someone in to change your sheets and bring you a fresh gown," Angela said. "Gucci or Prada?" she teased, no doubt trying to provide some much-needed leverage to the moment.

"Go with Gucci," Meghan said, playing along. "Black silk, with lace at the bosom. And a seam up the back would be nice."

Angela winked and smiled flirtatiously at Durk. "A gown like that, and you'd have your male sitter needing artificial respiration."

"And I'm sure Nurse Angela would be only

too happy to provide that service," Meghan teased once the nurse had left them alone.

"It's her duty," Durk said.

Meghan turned to Durk, actually taking a good look at him for the first time since he'd rushed to her nightmare rescue. He'd apparently gone home and showered and changed while she'd slept. He looked terrific. She, on the other hand, looked like a drowned, Hospital Barbie rip-off.

"I was definitely glad to see you walk through that door," Meghan said. "But you shouldn't have come back here tonight. You need some sleep. You probably have cows to take care of tomorrow."

"Don't worry. I'll doze in the chair. I can fall asleep anywhere, though I'm sure the cows are missing me."

But he couldn't keep spending all his days and nights with her. The real mystery was why he'd want to when she was only a woman he'd dated a few times two years ago.

The answer had to lie somewhere in her forgotten past.

In the meantime, she had to be careful not to fall for him. He hadn't found any reason to hang around two years ago. There was no reason to think he'd be any more interested now.

THE SHEETS WERE CRISP and unwrinkled. Meghan's gown was fresh and clean, though it was still a faded blue with an immodest opening in the back.

Durk was dozing in the more comfortable of the two chairs in the room, his head on the pillow, his stockinged feet propped on her bed.

Meghan was wide awake.

She thought of turning on the TV for late-night reruns of sitcoms taped before she was born, but she didn't want to disturb Durk.

Durk Lambert, her cowboy protector whom she knew almost nothing about. He was one more mystery in a world of the unknown. She had no reason to doubt him—or any real reason to trust him, except that he watched over her like a grizzly guarding a mischievous cub.

She reached for a fashion magazine that Durk had picked up for her in the hospital gift shop that afternoon. She thumbed through it quickly, barely glancing at the designer creations that graced every page.

The clothing in the publication didn't tempt her. She was far more interested in what hung in her closet. Was she as casual as Durk with his jeans and supersoft knit pullovers? Or did she go for the more chic fashion?

Did she sleep in worn tees and run out for the

morning paper in a ratty robe or did she go for slinky negligees? And most important of all, had she actually put herself out there as bait and lured a killer into her world?

Why would a P.I. with a reputation for being smart make such a tragic mistake?

There was little she could do tonight, but she was leaving the hospital in the morning with or without an official release. She still had a dull headache off and on, but she was no longer dizzy or nauseous and she was certain she'd aced the last half-dozen routine neuro checks—except for the memory tasks.

The memory would surely return soon. In the meantime, she could investigate herself and her actions over the last few days and weeks. She wasn't quite sure how she'd go about it, but she had no trouble using the television remote, operating the hospital bed or reading the hospital's menu of unappetizing meal options. So why not assume that her investigative skills would also come back to her as needed?

She got out of bed, went to the bathroom and then stopped to drape her extra blanket across Durk. She bent to straighten his boots and noticed an iPad jutting from his worn leather duffel.

He hadn't had it with him before so he'd obviously picked it up on his last trip home. She practically salivated in anticipation as she lifted the digital tablet from the duffel.

Endless, forgotten facts at her fingertips—unless Durk had the machine password protected so that she couldn't get onto the internet. That would be legitimate grounds for waking him from a sound sleep.

She flicked on the monitor as she climbed back into the bed. The screen lit up and rows of icons appeared. Once she was connected, she typed "Durk Lambert" in the search box and clicked.

Her efforts were instantly rewarded. She'd hit pay dirt.

She scanned the first dozen entries.

Durk Lambert addresses international oil executives.

Durk Lambert, a formidable CEO in the oil industry.

Durk Lambert to head national committee.

Durk Lambert attends meeting with congressional leaders.

Durk Lambert named the wealthiest and most eligible bachelor in Texas.

And in case there was any doubt they were talking about the Durk Lambert now sleeping with his stockinged feet propped on the foot of her bed, the last heading included pictures.

She clicked on a random article and began to read. The information boggled what was left of her memory-deficient mind. Her simple cowboy was anything but.

Not that he'd ever told her he was a cowboy, but when she'd called him one, he hadn't denied it and certainly hadn't seemed offended by it. How could she have guessed he was the CEO of a corporation worth billions?

She'd been completely unaware of his status, but she was certain no one else was. Certainly not Detective Smart or the nurses and techs who seemed to look for reasons to come into her room and check him out.

Dr. Levy must know, as well. Durk Lambert was as well-known in Dallas as the Cowboys or the grassy knoll.

Pulling her feet up Indian-style, she clicked on a collection of Durk Lambert photos. In most of them, he was not in jeans or boots, but in designer suits.

He was pictured with past and current presidents, dignitaries from around the world and with a large group of wounded servicemen who had apparently been hired by Lambert Inc. or its subsidiaries.

Last year he'd received the Texas Man of the Year Award. Last February the Bent Pine Ranch had bid and paid over half a million dollars for a grand champion steer raised by a fifteen-year-old physically handicapped boy.

Rich. Powerful. Influential. Magnanimous. Socially prominent. Incredibly handsome. That in a nutshell captured the essence of CEO Durk Lambert.

Strangely, it didn't begin to capture the essence of the protective and sensual man in his jeans and boots that she'd come to know over the last twenty-four hours. She set down the iPad and studied his profile in the soft, golden glow of her night-light.

He was snoring lightly, his chest rising and falling rhythmically, his shirt bunched under his chin, his chin dotted with dark whiskers. His family had billions and yet he was as natural as rain. No pretense. No affectation. No pompous demands.

He was the kind of man any woman would be thrilled to have park his boots under her bed. So why in the world had Meghan let him get away?

It seemed now that Meghan Sinclair was the real mystery. She changed the search to Meghan Sinclair, Dallas P.I.

It didn't talk long to figure out why Detective

Smart didn't trust her. It took even less time to realize that dozens of people had reason to want her dead.

She kept reading until her eyes grew heavy and she fell asleep with Durk's iPad still in her hands.

MEGHAN SAT ON the edge of the bed, trying to portray as much dignity and authority as she could while wearing a shapeless hospital gown and sporting a partially shaved, bandaged head.

"I appreciate your concern, Dr. Levy, but I'm not moving to a new room at Grantland Hospital."

"I know it's an inconvenience," he said. "But our telemetry beds are limited and you don't actually need one now. Other than the amnesia, you're making excellent progress."

"I know, which is why I'm leaving the hospital. As long as I don't participate in any strenuous activities, I should be fine. Many patients with concussions are released after twenty-four hours."

"Every patient is different, Meghan."

"I realize that, but I'm having fewer and fewer dizzy spells. I'm not nauseous. I ate and kept down a substantial meal last night and this morning. My headache is almost gone. And I'm

sure that I've passed all the recent miniscreen-
ings the nurses and techs have been conduct-
ing—well, except for the ones requiring memory
functions."

"That's true," Dr. Levy agreed, his tone and
manner suggesting he wasn't looking for a fight.
"But you had a serious concussion and you're
still feeling the effects of it. Your body must
have time to recover. That means rest and avoid-
ing stress for at least two weeks. If you don't get
that, the symptoms may persist and cause long-
lasting complications."

"I'll see that I get plenty of rest."

"If you don't, you could prolong the recovery process by weeks and that includes the amnesia."

"I certainly don't need that."

"No, you don't. My professional opinion is
that under the circumstances you need more hospital recovery time."

"What if she has someone with her at all
times?" Durk asked.

"Like a babysitter? No, thanks." Meghan
yanked the stupid droopy neckline of her disgusting gown back into place. "I don't need to be
spoon-fed. I just need a quiet place to stay until
I've fully regained my strength and memory."

"That won't be your condo," Durk said. "It's still off-limits by police order."

"Another bit of overkill," she said. "No one was murdered in my condo and physical attacks without life-threatening injuries don't necessarily warrant the crime scene being barricaded by the police."

Dr. Levy scribbled something on her chart. "You're a veritable wealth of information this morning, Meghan. Are you certain you haven't regained some of your memory?"

"She got hold of my iPad last night," Durk said. "I think she spent most of the night doing research."

"I can understand that," Dr. Levy said. "If I didn't remember who I was, I'd be trying to find out as much as I could, too. But if you were up half the night, you need to get some sleep today. I suggest we discuss your release again when I make afternoon rounds."

She shook her head. "I'm not staying another night. The hospital gives me nightmares."

"I suspect it's the situation that gives you nightmares," the doctor said.

But Meghan wasn't giving in. "I know my rights. Either you release me or I walk. All I need are the clothes I was wearing when I came in."

"Actually, the police took them as evidence. But I doubt you want them back. They were bloody and soiled with vomit."

She gagged a bit at the image. "I'll call Neiman's and have one of the clerks courier me over a new outfit."

Dr. Levy hugged the chart to his chest. "Why Neiman's?"

"I have an account there and—" She stopped mid-sentence. "I do have an account with them. At least I think I do. I wouldn't know that unless I was starting to get my memory back, would I?"

"Not likely."

Meghan's optimism soared. "This changes everything," she said. "Even you have to admit that there's no reason for me to spend another day in the hospital now."

"Actually, it doesn't change my mind, but I'll consider releasing you today if you convince me that you have somewhere nonstressful to go and someone to keep an eye on you."

"I have a three-bedroom condo in downtown Dallas," Durk said.

"I'm not moving in with you, Durk Lambert."

"It was just a suggestion."

The answer was no for too many reasons to count, including the fact that she didn't trust herself to be alone with him for any length of time. She already found him attractive and that was with a trauma-weakened libido.

Of course, she looked like Queen of the Zombies with her botched hair and bruised face. So obviously, this was not about sex for Durk.

"I have the perfect solution," Durk said.

"So do I," Meghan countered. "It's called a hotel. I'm a successful private investigator. I must have money somewhere. I'll just have to track down information on what bank I use and what credit cards I have. And I should at least check out the damage to my condo. And see when Ben's funeral will be held."

"I wish you would hear and see yourself, Meghan. You're already exhibiting symptoms of nervousness and guaranteeing stress." Dr. Levy turned to Durk. "What is your perfect solution?"

"Meghan can stay at the Bent Pine Ranch. She can have a private suite with a computer for her research and plenty of time and space to relax. I'll hire a nurse to oversee her recovery."

A nurse following her around every second. She'd go nuts.

But the idea of a private suite didn't sound half bad—except... "Who else lives on the ranch? You said your whole family lives there. Are you sure you'd have room?"

"It's a very big house."

He wasn't exaggerating. She'd read and seen pictures of the house and ranch online last night. It was a working ranch with a huge sprawling home that had sheltered generations of Lamberts.

Several thousand head of cattle grazed the acres and acres of fenced pasture land. Their stables housed quarter horses, Appaloosas and Tennessee walkers. And the ranch had endless hiking and riding trails along Beaver Creek and Indian Ridge.

"I know Carolina Lambert quite well," Dr. Levy said. "If you agree to spend a week at the Bent Pine Ranch, I'll feel comfortable releasing you from the hospital."

And in spite of what she claimed, Meghan did still need Durk's help, at least until she could drive again.

"Okay, Durk. I haven't the faintest idea why you're choosing to get involved in this, but if you get approval from your family, I'll stay at the ranch for a week—as long as we can stop by my condo and pick up some of my things on the way out of town."

"Are you sure you wouldn't rather just stop at Neiman Marcus?"

"I'm certain. Crossing the police barrier to

enter my own condo doesn't bother me in the least."

"Then we have a deal."

Dr. Levy gave her dismissal instructions, including how to tend the head wound and when to come back and have the staples removed.

She opted to borrow Durk's trench-style raincoat until she could choose something to wear from her own closet. When they were ready to leave, she wrapped herself in it and cinched it tightly since she was wearing absolutely nothing underneath.

Durk waited with her for the wheelchair the nurse insisted she ride in to Durk's car—hospital rules. It was as good a time as any to get a few things off her mind.

"Why did you let me go on believing you were a simple cowboy, Durk?"

"You never said you thought I was simple. I would have called you on that. But I am a cowboy."

"You're a businessman. I bet you haven't touched a cow in years, much less branded one."

"You'd be wrong on both counts. I help out on the ranch every chance I get. It helps keep me sane, and I love working alongside my brothers. I think of myself as every bit a cowboy as they are."

"Why?"

"Because being a cowboy is more than branding a steer or stamping through cow patties. It's a creed that affects every aspect of our lives."

"What kind of creed?"

"The unspoken rules we live by. A cowboy does what has to be done and he does it well. He's a man of his word. If he makes a promise he keeps it. He's respectful of women. He has a passion for wide-open spaces. Though he didn't teach it as a list of rules, Dad made sure that my brothers and I understood them. Mom made sure we lived them until they were as much a part of us as breathing."

"You're serious, aren't you?"

"As serious as I get."

"Is that creed why you're standing by me now?"

"I don't know why I'm here, Meghan. I honestly don't know. But right now this is what I have to do and this is where I want to be."

That was reason enough for now.

THIRTY MINUTES LATER, Durk parked his Jaguar in the parking garage attached to Meghan's condo complex. As she stepped out and onto the pavement, anxiety pitted in her stomach and sent an icy blast through her veins.

Durk put a hand on the small of her back. "Are you sure you're ready for this?"

"No, but I have to go through with it."

"Somehow I knew you would."

Chapter Ten

Durk followed Meghan onto the elevator. He could tell she was nervous but it didn't keep her from noticing every security camera they'd passed and commenting on the key card entrance to every door.

When the elevator doors closed, she reached out to the keypad and punched five. The move surprised him.

"Strange that you don't remember the complex, but you just punched the button for the fifth floor."

She looked puzzled. "What number should I have punched?"

"Five. I just didn't expect you to know that."

He was starting to wonder if Smart could be right about her faking the amnesia so that she could go after the killer herself. Blurring the lines between her job and the police's had always been her modus operandi.

Meghan stepped to the back of the elevator. "I guess punching the number is ingrained like using a computer or doing the other everyday things I do without thinking."

That was one explanation. When they exited the elevator, he stood back, watching to see which direction she chose. She started walking toward her condo at a brisk pace, then stopped as if she'd forgotten something.

She turned back to him. "Where do I go from here?"

"Keep walking. It's the last door on the right."

She slowed and waited on him to fall in step with her. "How is it you came to keep a key to the parking garage entrance and my condo when we broke up?"

"You never asked for them back."

"And I didn't change the lock. Apparently I trusted you. Then again, your family owns half of Dallas, so it wasn't like you'd sneak in and steal my silver."

"I don't recall you having any silver. Now had I been into ladies' shoes…"

"Great. I have shoes. I can shed these horrid slippers you bought me."

"The woman in the hospital gift shop said they were all the rage."

"For six-year-olds."

"That's why real men don't buy women's shoes."

The lightness was all staged and not working. Meghan's muscles visibly tensed and her pace slowed to a crawl as they neared the end of the hallway.

"The police tape is gone," she said as they reached her door.

"Thoughtful of Smart," Durk said. "Now you won't even be breaking the law when you open your own door."

"It wasn't the detective's idea."

Durk spun around at the voice. An attractive young woman in a dark blue fitted suit stood in the doorway just across the hall. A dog almost as tall as she was strained to break away from her fingers that clutched his studded collar.

"Settle down, Bitsy. These are our new neighbors." Bitsy continued to strain to break free.

"My husband is the mayor's brother," the woman explained. "He had his brother pull a few strings. We're having my whole family down from Memphis for Thanksgiving. They're arriving tomorrow and, let's face it, the tape made this look like we'd moved into a ghetto."

"So you're new here?" Meghan asked.

"Yes. Sara Cunningham. And you have to be Meghan Sinclair."

"The bruises and bandages wouldn't let me deny it if I wanted to. This is Durk," she said, nodding his way.

"Are you two married or…"

"We're friends," Meghan answered.

"I'd heard you were single and that you were a famous P.I. Our neighbor, Bill, said he was the one who came to your rescue when you were attacked."

"Yes, and I haven't had a chance to thank him."

"As soon as I heard, it changed my mind about wanting to live here, but we'd already signed the paperwork. So, here we are."

"I wouldn't worry about the attack," Meghan said. "I'm sure it wasn't random."

"That's what your brother said."

Durk had already unlocked the door and his hand was on the doorknob. He let go of it and stepped back into the hall. "Did you say you'd talked to Meghan's brother?"

"Yes. He was here yesterday morning, really early, before my husband went to work. He was super friendly and it was sweet how concerned he was about you, Meghan. My brother was never that caring."

Confusion shadowed Meghan's face. "Are you certain he said he was my brother?"

"Absolutely. He said he was here to pick up some things you needed in the hospital. He must have brought them to you."

"No, I don't think—"

"It could have been your brother," Durk interrupted, keeping his voice steady and his tone nonchalant. He needed to keep Sara talking. One inkling on her part that she'd talked to the killer and she'd clam up before he could blink.

"I can tell for sure if it was him or not," Durk bragged. "What did he look like?"

"He was nice-looking. Tall, but maybe not quite as tall as you. Light brown hair. Not heavy-set but not thin, either. Kind of average. I don't mean that in a bad way."

"That sounds like him," Meghan agreed, quickly picking up on Durk's motives. "I was kind of out of it yesterday. I'm sure I saw him and just don't remember it. Did he stay long at the condo?"

"I don't know. I didn't see what time he got here. I just saw him leave. He had some files you needed."

That explained his visit.

"Was he dressed for the office," Durk asked, "or was he wearing those grungy jeans he wears on his day off?"

"He didn't look grungy." She put a finger to

her cheek as if she were trying to remember. "He looked good. Muscular. Nice personality, well-spoken. But he's scared of dogs. You should have seen how upset he was when Bitsy jumped up to give him a kiss." A phone rang inside Sara's condo.

"Sorry," Sara said. "That's probably the furniture store with my dining room table. We'll need it for Thanksgiving Day. I have to buzz them up. Nice to meet both of you, and I hope you get better soon, Meghan."

She disappeared inside her own condo before Durk could question her more. But he figured he'd already gotten as much out of the new neighbor as she knew.

The attacker had been here before Durk yesterday. His return had been risky, so he must have been desperate to retrieve specific files.

"I don't have a brother, do I?" Meghan asked.

"Not that I've ever heard you mention."

"So it had to be Ben's killer that Sara met."

"That would be my theory."

Durk couldn't help but note that since he'd told Meghan about Ben, her concern had totally shifted from the attack on her to his murder. And this was when she had no memory of him.

"The killer's nervy," she said. "And overly confident. That would suggest he's either gotten away with murder before or he thinks he's smarter than me or the police."

Her P.I. skills were kicking in. That worried him. He knew firsthand what she was like when she was on someone's trail. Only this time her reasoning and body might not be up to the task. He had to get her out of Dallas and down to the ranch where he could protect her from the killer and herself.

"There's no proof as yet that your attacker killed Ben," he reminded her.

"But there are valid reasons to suspect it."

Meghan pushed open the door and stepped into her condo.

He worried that the sight of the chaos on top of everything else might push her over the edge. Instead he heard the voice of the Meghan of old.

"Somebody's head is going to roll for this."

"I warned you that the place was a mess."

"This is more than a mess. It's a train wreck." Meghan stooped and picked up a piece of the shattered glass from the broken lamp. She turned it over several times in her hand before finally dropping it back to the floor to glisten among the other gem-like shards.

She trailed her hand through a buildup of fingerprint dust and then stared at the back wall. "And that must be my blood." She touched the edge of her bandage with the tips of her fingers. "You'd think if I were such a hotshot P.I. I'd know how to defend myself."

"You're alive," Durk said. "You must have done something right."

"I screamed for help and had the good fortune to have a neighbor who was willing to come to my rescue. Good thing I was attacked before the weekend. I might have ruined Sara's party." Her voice broke as the forced bravado wore thin.

Impulsively, Durk slipped his arms around her waist. The touch instantly fanned the flames of desire he'd been trying so desperately to ignore.

He let his arms drop back to his side and stepped away from her. "Do you want to call Detective Smart and tell him your *brother* stopped by for a visit?"

"Not yet. He's already indicated he doesn't want me to do his job for him."

"And he's right. You need to let him handle this investigation. Getting your strength and memory back is enough for you to deal with right now."

"Right," she said without a hint of conviction.

She turned slowly, studying the mess from every angle. "There's a silver clutch on the coffee table, open, obviously already examined by the cops and maybe my attacker, as well."

"I doubt the attacker got the chance once your neighbor showed up."

Meghan dropped to the couch and went through the small bag's contents. A tube of bright red lipstick, a mirrored compact, a tissue and two twenty dollar bills. Her spirits fell. "No phone. No car keys. No scribbled name or phone numbers."

"The phone and keys could still be around here somewhere." Durk took out his cell phone and called her number from memory. The phone rang six times before a computerized voice said the connection could not be made at this time. He repeated the message for Meghan.

Her hands flew up in frustration. "The murdering slime has my phone."

"You're jumping to conclusions."

"Reasonable conclusions."

"I can't argue that, except we're not even sure at this point that I called your number. You could have changed to a new number in the last two years. But I do think we should call Smart," Durk said. "If your phone is in the perp's possession, the cops should be able to use it to track him down."

"I'm sure Smart is already on that," Meghan said. "In the meantime, the murderous rat's probably already stolen any information I had stored on the phone."

"Knowing you, your phone is the latest and smartest available and enhanced to guarantee your info is secure."

"I'll still have it disconnected."

"First, we should make certain that was your current number and that the phone isn't here."

"If it were here, I would have heard it ring."

"Not if the battery has run down. Shall we start the search in your home office?"

"I have a home office?"

"You have a desk and shelves upon shelves of true crime books."

"Lead the way. Wait. Is that a dead cat under that chair by the window?"

Durk dropped to his knees and rescued a wig in a shade of blond previously unknown to mankind. He tossed it to her. "You've just embarrassed every cat in the world."

Meghan held it up in front of her. "Was I a P.I. and a hooker?"

"Now you're insulting hookers."

She set the floozy wig on the chair. It was time for real work to begin.

ONE LOOK AT THE open drawers of the desk and the files that had been rifled and left askew and

Meghan knew their quest was futile. The killer had come back and taken everything that could have possibly tied him to the crimes.

She bit back tears of frustration as the nagging headache set in again. Even though nothing looked familiar to her, she felt violated. It was her condo, after all. This was the space that should be her haven.

Instead it had been contaminated and turned into just another disjointed faction of her perplexing existence.

Durk was the only constant in her life, and even he was temporary. They'd had their go at a relationship and failed, a relationship she couldn't even remember.

She studied the pictures on the wall, nighttime scenes of Dallas area landmarks. Cowboys Stadium. Reunion Tower. The John F. Kennedy Memorial. All more familiar to her than her own home.

Durk looked up from the files he was perusing. "Here's a recent copy of your phone bill. You do have the same number you had when we were dating."

"Good. Give me the bill. Now I can at least talk to the company and request a printout of all the calls made to and from my phone for the last month."

Durk handed her the bill and his cell phone.

After being transferred to three different representatives, she finally got the definitive answer. And now she was really ready to boil.

"That didn't seem to go well," Durk said.

"They can't provide me with a printout because the DPD has blocked the account. The police are now the only ones with access to the records."

"Don't worry about that. I'll find a way to get a list. Do you still have Smart's business card?"

She reached into the trench coat pocket. "I do. Why?"

"I'm giving him a call to see what's going on with your phone. If he has it, it's possible he also has your laptop."

"Put it on speaker," she said. "We'll make it a conference call."

Smart answered on the second ring.

"Durk Lambert. Speak of the devil. Sorry, make that the Good Samaritan. I understand from Dr. Levy that you're providing our friend Meghan with a week in the Bent Pine Recovery Center."

"I'm also on the line," Meghan said. "So you might want to keep your comments about me on a professional level."

"Hello, Meghan. Nice to hear from you, but I

would have thought you'd give me a call before you left the hospital."

"I had nothing new to share with you. I've told you everything I know until the amnesia runs its course."

"So what can I help you with now?"

"My laptop is missing and I can't locate my cell phone or my car keys. Do you have them?"

"No. When police searched your condo and your office yesterday afternoon, they didn't find computers or cell phones in either place."

"Yet you found her office answering machine with the strange message intact?" Durk commented.

"We questioned that, as well, but the killer must have simply overlooked it."

"Or he intentionally left it there for you to find that message."

"That's also possible."

"I just called my service provider," Meghan said. "They told me my account had been blocked by order of the DPD."

"I made that decision after realizing your phone was likely in the hands of the attacker."

"How did you come to that conclusion?"

"We tracked the location of the phone."

"Are you saying you tracked it to the killer?" Durk asked.

"Unfortunately, no. We found the phone in the middle of a soccer field in Garland. It's busted up pretty bad, but you can have it back if you like."

"I'd like," Meghan said, though she had no idea what good it would do her now.

"I'll send someone by your office to pick it up," Durk volunteered. "What about Meghan's car? Do you have any idea what happened to it?"

"No, only that it's not in the condo parking garage.But we checked your registration, Meghan. We've put out a description of the car and the license plate number. Every law enforcement officer in the state is on the lookout for it."

"What kind of vehicle do I own?"

"A silver Mercedes, this year's model. Hopefully, we'll find it with our perp behind the wheel."

"I hope the same."

Smart stressed again that she should call if she remembered anything at all that might help ID the suspect.

When the call ended, Meghan dropped to a modern chair that she'd obviously chosen for style over comfort. She massaged her neck and tried to break the tension that was tightening her muscles.

"You're running out of steam," Durk said.

"Go throw together a few items of clothing and let's get out of here. Next stop, the Bent Pine Ranch and a long nap for you."

The Bent Pine Ranch and a man she was growing more attached to by the second. A gorgeous, rugged, hunk of a cowboy CEO who had once been her lover. She dared not think of what would happen when those memories returned.

MEGHAN WAS RELIEVED to find that the bedroom held no new discouraging surprises. The beautiful Tiffany lamps that bracketed the king-size bed were intact. A few of the drawers in an antique chest were ajar, but no clothes were scattered about the floor.

The sleigh bed with its snowy-white coverlet and multitude of pillows looked so tempting, it was all she could do not to crawl into it and sink into the luxury.

Meghan walked to the closet and started to open the door. A shiver of dread stopped her. Suppose she opened the door to yet another nightmare? Like a body. The hairs on the back of her neck rose. Goose bumps broke out on her arms.

This was ridiculous. She couldn't play into this kind of crippling fear. She would not be intimidated by her own home.

She yanked the door open and stared into a roomy walk-in closet. Nothing but rows of clothes, all neatly coordinated.

And there were shoes—dozens of pairs in every color and style displayed on a revolving floor-to-ceiling built-in rack. She kicked out of the horrid slippers in anticipation. Her feet sank into the thick carpet as she picked up a pair of strappy black heels. This was more like it.

She untied the trench coat and stepped out of it. She knew Durk couldn't see her, but just knowing she was in the nude while he was nearby made her feel risqué.

She blushed to realize the feeling didn't overly distress her. She padded to the antique chest and opened drawers until she found the one that held her underwear.

Thankfully, there were no granny panties in sight, but there were lots of silky bikini briefs and thong panties in a variety of colors. Apparently, P.I. Meghan Sinclair had her sexy side. Perhaps that was what had lured Durk into a relationship with her in the first place.

She chose a pair of black silk panties to wear under her jeans. She slipped into them and a black lacy bra and then went back to the closet for her jeans. Once she'd wiggled into them, she chose an emerald-green V-neck sweater and pulled it over her head.

She flicked through the hangers quickly. She filled a garment bag with her selections and then dropped to the edge of the bed. Fatigue was setting in and with it the dizziness that had plagued her all day yesterday.

Dr. Levy had warned her about doing too much too soon. Another day in the hospital might have been a good idea, except that being confined was maddening and that couldn't be good for her, either.

She just needed to slow down. Pack simply.

Almost done, she went back and checked the bottom drawer of the chest, the only one she hadn't opened. There were stacks of scarves, gloves, belts and hats. Picking up one of the jaunty, knit newsboy hats, she plopped it on her head and went to check out the results in the mirror that hung over the marble-topped dresser.

To her surprise, the hat was actually flattering, the perfect cover for the bandage and short, spiky hairs that crept from the edge of the bandage.

She looked around, still feeling like she was forgetting something. When she spotted the jewelry box, she decided to take one quick look inside.

A small gold locket on a chain caught her eye. She picked it up and let the filigreed chain curl around her left hand as her fingers caressed the smooth, flawless locket.

She loosed the clasp and opened the locket. Her mother smiled back at her from the tiny, heart-shaped photo. Her mother and yet the only reason Meghan recognized her was from the snapshots Durk had shown her at the hospital.

Unwanted tears welled in the corners of her eyes. Meghan fought them for as long as she could before giving in to sobs and a crush of emotions she could no longer distinguish or control.

Durk joined her in the bedroom, walking up and standing behind her. "What's wrong?"

"This." She handed him the locket without turning around. She watched his reflection in the mirror as he studied her mother's picture.

He put a hand on her shoulder. "Are you crying because you can remember her?"

"No," she whispered. "I'm crying because I can't."

He slipped the delicate chain around her neck and fastened it. She trembled at the coolness of the locket against her breast and the heat of Durk's breath on the back of her neck.

His left hand clasped her shoulder. The fingers

of his right hand trailed the chain and straightened the locket until it was perfectly centered in the swell of her cleavage.

The tears had stopped. Her pulse quickened. Without warning, she became so light-headed she had to hold on to the dresser for support.

Durk lifted her hair from her neck and his lips touched the bared flesh.

Her breath caught and held as titillating sensations zinged along her nerve endings.

She closed her eyes to savor the sensation. When she opened them, Durk had backed away.

"We should get going," he said, his voice huskier than it had been before. "If you're through packing, I can carry your bags to the car."

"No need," she said. "Both bags are wheeled. There's nothing to carry."

"I made a few calls while you were packing," Durk said. "A list of calls made to and from your cell phone during the previous thirty days will be faxed to you at the ranch. It should be there by nightfall."

"That was fast. Money and influence obviously get results."

"I just happen to have the right connections."

"I'm sure. Do you always get what you want, CEO Lambert?"

He met her gaze. There was something in the

depths of his whiskey-colored eyes she hadn't noticed before. Pain or perhaps resolve. Or regret.

"No, Meghan. I don't always get what I want."

FIVE MINUTES LATER, bags zipped and waiting at the door with Durk, Meghan made one last trip through the condo, praying that something—anything—would scratch a nerve and shake the lost memories free.

When nothing did, she walked back to the bedroom for her handbag. And for some reason she didn't want to think about, she opened a drawer, grabbed a silky red chemise, wrapped it in a scarf and tucked it in the bottom of her purse.

Her intercom buzzed just as Meghan was about to pull the door closed behind them. "I should get that, though I won't know who's waiting at the building entrance even after they tell me."

She pushed the talk button. "Can I help you?"

"You can if this is Meghan Sinclair."

"Who is this?"

"Connie."

"I'm sorry. I'm drawing a blank."

"Connie, you know? Connie Latimer. I hired

you to find out who killed my sister. The cops aren't even looking anymore."

"And that's why you hired me."

"Yes. I'd heard you were the best person in Texas at finding evidence the police hadn't discovered. Just last week you said you were getting really close to having what you needed to get this man arrested."

"What else did I tell you?"

"Nothing else. But then when I heard on the news that you were assaulted and your assistant was killed, I panicked. I mean, I know what that guy did to my sister. I know what he's capable of."

"I'm fine, Connie, but unfortunately, I don't have any further information to give you concerning the case."

"But remember that you thought he'd killed more than one woman?"

"I recall that," she lied, in order to keep Connie talking.

"Well, I think he killed another one down in Houston just a few days ago."

Meghan took a deep breath and exhaled slowly. "In that case, Connie, I'm glad you're here. We definitely need to talk."

Chapter Eleven

Meghan watched as Durk walked back to join her and Connie at one of the coffee shop's outdoor tables. His easy cowboy swagger paired well with his charismatic charm. He slid the two steamy cappuccinos he carried in front of Meghan and Connie and kept the black coffee for himself.

Thankfully, they had the patio area to themselves. The storm that had ridden in on the tail of her nightmare last night had given way to chilly temperatures and occasional wind gusts that kept the other customers inside.

Continuing their discussion at the coffee shop across from the condo had been Durk's suggestion, but Meghan had quickly consented. Meeting a client at the scene of her brutal assault could have been unsettling for Connie.

It might have even frightened her into silence, especially considering the way Connie was staring at her bruises and head bandage. She should have kept her hat on, but she'd been afraid the wind would send it sailing.

"I'm sorry about the attack," Connie said. "The guy really did a number on you."

"Yes, he did. But I'm going to be fine in a few days," Meghan assured her. Meghan uncrossed her legs and pulled her chair closer to the table. "I'm going to level with you, Connie. I don't remember talking to you last week. I actually don't recall anything about the case."

Connie's face registered alarm. "But you said this was almost over. You practically guaranteed me that the arrest of the man who killed Roxanne was imminent. You used the word *imminent*. I'm sure of it."

"I believe you, and I'm sure I didn't lie to you. But I suffered a serious concussion from the attack. It's temporarily affected my memory."

Connie's brow knitted. "Then you don't even know what I'm talking about."

"*Temporary* is the operative word here," Durk said. "The doctor expects a full recovery of Meghan's memory."

"When?"

"At any time," Meghan assured her. "But for now, I need your help in getting up to full speed on the case."

"Where do I start?"

"At the beginning. Give me a quick review of the events leading up to Roxanne's murder."

"You have this in your files."

"I'd like to hear it from you." Especially since Meghan had no relevant files in her immediate possession. "But you can keep it concise."

Connie's gaze remained downcast as she toyed with the handle of her cup. "I thought people only had amnesia in books and movies."

"So did I," Meghan said. "But trust me, retrograde amnesia occurs in real life, as well."

"I have to trust you. You're my only hope."

"So tell me about Roxanne."

Connie sucked her bottom lip in her mouth, hesitated and then finally sat up straight and started talking.

"It was two years ago next January. Roxanne was in her freshman year at UT. It was a Thursday night near the end of her first semester. She'd gone out with some girlfriends to let off steam after a chemistry final."

"Did they go to a friend's house or to a bar?"

"They went to a pub near the university. They'd been there before. Her friends said Roxanne was laughing and drinking and seemed to be having fun. Then all of a sudden she told them she had a headache and that she was going back to the dorm."

Connie picked up a spoon and stirred her beverage, staring at the swirling foam. "That was the last time anyone ever saw my sister alive."

Meghan hated putting Connie through the heartbreaking task of repeating the events yet again, but it couldn't be helped.

"Did anything unusual happen prior to your sister's abrupt headache?" Durk asked.

"Nothing anyone could recall."

"No confrontation with anyone? No phone calls? No text messages?"

"One of her friends said she had seen Roxanne take out her phone and check her messages a few minutes earlier, but she didn't seem upset."

"Did the police check her phone for texts and messages?"

"They couldn't. Roxanne's phone never turned up again. Neither did her computer."

A missing phone. A missing computer. Missing evidence that might have linked the killer to the crime. But those similarities in themselves were not unusual and definitely not enough to link Roxanne's killer to Ben.

But the additional evidence Meghan had discovered might—if she could only remember it. She struggled to choke back the aggravation before it hindered her ability to absorb all of what Connie had to say.

"What happened next?" Durk asked, keeping them on track.

"When her friends got back to the dorm and discovered Roxanne wasn't there, they became concerned. But they figured she could have hooked up with a guy and didn't want them to know about it. Then when she hadn't returned by the next morning, they became really worried."

"So she wasn't reported as missing until the following morning?" Meghan asked.

"Right, and even then, I think the police just figured she was hanging out with other friends—or a guy. It wasn't until late that afternoon that one of her friends finally contacted my mother. She got in touch with the police right away and demanded they start looking for Roxanne."

"How long was it before they found the body?" Meghan asked.

"Two weeks, but the autopsy showed that she'd been dead less than twenty-four hours when they pulled her car out of a flooding creek with her in it. The monster had held her prisoner, repeatedly raping her while he slowly starved her to death."

Connie buried her face in her hands. When

she looked up, her eyes were wet with tears. "I want her killer found, Ms. Sinclair. I don't care what it takes. He didn't just kill Roxanne. He killed our mother, too. She had a stroke two days after ID'ing Roxanne's emaciated body."

"That must have been really hard on you."

"It's still hard, especially since I know the cops have given up. And there's one more thing."

"What's that?"

"When they found Roxanne's body, she was dressed in a weird outfit that I know didn't belong to her."

"You mean like a costume?"

"No, more like a little girl's dress. It was short, ruffled and buttoned to the neck. I'm not explaining this well, but it was like something they wore in the old days."

Meghan must have set herself up as bait to lure Roxanne's killer into a trap. Only somehow he'd found out and her plan had backfired.

That could explain the stun gun. It would have rendered her helpless but kept her alive. Then he could have tortured her the way he'd tortured Roxanne.

"Was there anything else unusual about Roxanne's appearance?"

"Her face was smeared with bright red lipstick and her hair had been dyed a platinum blond."

The red lipstick in Meghan's handbag, the hideous wig in her condo. They could be connected, indicators that her assailant, Roxanne's killer and Ben's assassin were one and the same.

Meghan's heart raced. She knew who the killer was. She'd tracked him down. Only now his identity had been sucked into the dead zone of her mind.

"If we don't do something, Roxanne will never get justice," Connie said. "And the monster will just go on killing."

Connie pulled a folded page from the morning newspaper from her purse and shoved it in front of Meghan.

Meghan scanned the article that Connie had highlighted. A car containing an unidentified woman's emaciated body had been pulled from a swollen river south of Houston.

"May I keep the article?" Meghan asked.

"If you think it will help."

"It could." She passed the newspaper to Durk.

Meghan grew restless as he read it. She pushed her coffee away as strings of seemingly unconnected images began to explode in her mind with dizzying force.

Durk's voice cut through the chaos. "Meghan, are you all right?"

"I'm dizzy." Her stomach lurched. "And I think I'm going to be sick."

"I've upset her," Connie said. "I'd better go."

"I think so," Durk said. "She'll get back to you."

Beads of cold sweat trickled down Meghan's bosom. Her vision blurred. Objects swirled around her.

The next thing Meghan knew Durk was placing her into the passenger seat of his car.

She looked up. His expression was grim and worried.

She swallowed hard. "Did I black out?"

"I'll say you did. One minute you were fine, the next you were slumped over in your chair."

"You carried me all the way to the car?"

"It was only a few steps."

"I'm sorry."

"Don't apologize. I'm just thankful you're talking sensibly again."

"How long was I out?"

"Probably less than a minute, but it seemed a lot longer. You scared me half to death."

"What happened to Connie?"

"She went home, but she scribbled her phone number on a napkin and stuck it in my pocket while I was carrying you to the car."

"Good. I'll call her later—when I can remember her sister's killer. Right now, I'm just ready to get out of Dallas. How far is it to your ranch?"

"We're not going to the ranch. We're going back to the hospital."

"No way." She defied the nausea and sat up straight, glaring at him as he crawled into the driver's seat. "I'm not going back to the hospital."

"Meghan, you just fainted back there."

"I was only out for a few seconds and that was because of a dizzy spell. I'm fine now. And I don't think what just happened was necessarily a bad thing."

"Then you have a strange way of evaluating events."

"A dizzy spell is not an event, Durk. It's a minor side effect. The good thing is that I think my memory is on the verge of a comeback. While you were scanning that newspaper article, images started colliding in my mind like disjointed fragments of my life."

"Colliding images in your head does not sound like progress to me."

"It could be—if the images help me remember. Besides, the doctor said I should expect some continued dizziness and nausea."

"He didn't mention fainting."

"He didn't know the kind of morning I was going to have."

"Exactly. You were supposed to be resting at the Bent Pine."

"And I will be, as soon as you get me there."

"You can rest at the hospital. It's closer."

"No one ever rests at a hospital. Look at me, Durk. I'm fine. I had a dizzy spell. That's all."

He backed out of the parking spot. "I can't look at you. I'm driving."

"Then *listen* to me. Take me to the ranch. We made a deal. And you said you're a man of your word. It's part of the cow creed."

"The *cowboy* creed. And so is protecting animals, children and women who are too stubborn to listen to reason."

"I promise I'll spend the rest of the day relaxing. That's exactly what they'd have me do at the hospital except that every time I fell asleep someone would come in to see what I wanted for lunch or tell me to track the movement of their finger or poke me or want to change my bed or—"

"I get the picture. And speaking of lunch, you haven't had any. You could probably use some food in your stomach."

She wasn't quite that fine. "Why don't we wait until we're out of the city traffic?"

"If we're going to do that, we may as well have lunch at the ranch."

"I don't want to cause extra work for anyone."

"You have a lot to learn about life at the Bent Pine."

"I guess you have a full staff of servants."

"Oh, yeah. You don't even have to breathe for yourself if you don't want to bother."

That might be an exaggeration, but she could well imagine that none of the Lambert women ever stepped into the kitchen unless it was to approve a menu.

"I'll have nothing to do at the ranch but rest and recuperate in the lap of luxury."

"But you won't. You'll do nothing but fret over killers and try to figure out a way to do Detective Smart's job for him."

"That's my job, the same as running an oil company is yours. You know you don't leave the problems and complications behind you every day at five."

"I might if I was recovering from a concussion. But a deal is a deal. I'm willing to go straight to the ranch if you promise me that you'll spend the remainder of the day resting."

"Rest doesn't mean staying in bed all day."

"Suit yourself, but if you pass out again, I'm calling Dr. Levy. If he says you need to return to the hospital, you will—if I have to hog-tie you and drag you back myself."

She'd like to see him try it. But not now. She really was tired and still a bit nauseous. Still, she had to level with him. Once she did, he might no longer want her at his family ranch.

"I'm almost certain that the madman who tortured and killed Roxanne is the same man who attacked me and killed Ben. I must have been close to having the evidence I needed to have him arrested and he somehow found out I was just luring him into a trap."

"That explains a few things," Durk said. "Like why he didn't shoot you in the head the way he did Ben. He had other plans for you."

"But why kill Ben with my gun? If he'd planned to kill him all along, he must have had his own weapon."

"Maybe he liked the irony."

"What irony?"

"That by not going to the police with your evidence sooner, by limiting all information suggesting him as a prime suspect to the private files shared only by you and Ben, you provided the motive for him to kill Ben."

"I was obviously still acquiring evidence necessary for an arrest and a conviction."

"And you don't like sharing the credit for that with cops."

"You don't know that."

"Are you going to tell Detective Smart about your conversation with Connie Latimer?"

"I'll think about it."

"I rest my case. But it's your life. I'm just here as a friend."

His insinuations were troubling, but that didn't mean he was right. She closed her eyes. She was too tired to deal with this now.

Next stop: Lambert World.

And a week with a man who could thrill her with his touch or heap on recriminations with his words.

And somewhere beyond the barbed fences of Bent Pine Ranch was a killer whose freedom depended on her not remembering his name.

DURK STOOD NEAR THE back of his low-slung sports car, his phone to his ear while the tank filled with fuel. "We should be there in about thirty minutes," he said when his mother finally answered.

"You told me that an hour ago. What delayed you?"

"It's a long story, but it's been a busier morning than I'd expected."

"Well, at least you're on your way now. I freshened the guest suite and Alexis stopped at the florist in Oak Grove when she took Tommy in for a haircut. She found the most beautiful fall blossoms. I just finished arranging them. They'll really brighten the guest room."

"I'm sure Meghan will appreciate that."

"Alexis is especially excited about seeing Meghan again. Apparently they got to know each other pretty well while Meghan was working with her and Tague."

"I'm sure they'll have plenty of time to hang out and chat but maybe not today. Meghan is going to need lots of rest."

"I'll do what I can to see that she has peace and quiet."

"About that. I'd like to hire around-the-clock private nurses for a couple of days."

"That won't be a problem. The Carsons' oldest daughter manages a home-duty private nurse register. When I called her about help with Sybil, she recommended a young RN who is willing to stay here at the ranch."

Two patients. He could kick himself for forgetting to even ask about his aunt. That's how worried Meghan had him. "How is Aunt Sybil?"

"A bit demanding. I think she's reveling in the attention. But she's responding well to the medication. Her breathing is easier and her appetite is almost back to normal."

"Speaking of appetites, neither Meghan nor I have had lunch. Do you—"

"I'll take care of it, don't you fret." He knew his mom would. "You know, Durk, this caretaker side of you is one I've never seen before. I like it."

"Don't get too used to it. When Meghan's memory returns, she's on her own."

"Still, Meghan must be a very special woman. I can't wait to meet her."

"Don't make any bonds you can't break. She's here for a week or less. Then it's *adios*."

"We'll see."

But Durk had already seen. Meghan turned him on. There was no doubt about that. But no matter how hot the lust and desire, he would not let himself get romantically involved with her again.

He was absolutely crazy about her, but nothing had changed. He had no reason to believe it ever would.

MEGHAN WOKE TO the sound of a slamming car door. She stretched, opened her eyes and stared in amazement at the sprawling ranch house.

It vaguely resembled the picture of the house

she'd seen on the internet. The gables were there. So were the multiple chimneys and the wide front porch.

But the house that had been featured in a Texas magazine had looked far more elegant and pretentious. There had been giant gaslights leading to the house and a garden in front that looked as if it had jumped from a Monet painting. Even the columns had looked larger and far more impressive in the photograph.

Durk appeared and opened her car door. The straps from her two pieces of luggage were slung across his shoulder. "Welcome to the Bent Pine Ranch."

She slipped her feet back into the high heels she'd kicked out of earlier and stepped out of the car. "Is this where you live?"

"It is whenever I can escape the city. Just breathe that good, clean air—mixed with cow manure, of course. Had you been awake for the quarter of a mile, you would have seen some of the finest Angus cattle in Texas."

She was still dumbstruck by the house. There wasn't one indication that the owners were one of the richest families in Texas.

"Is this really where your family lives?"

"Yep. This is home. See that big oak tree over

by the fence?" He pointed her in the right direction.

"What about it?"

"I got my first broken leg falling out of it when it was five."

"You say that like you've had lots of broken legs."

"Only two. That's all the legs I have." He chuckled. "But I've broken one of them twice."

"Falling from trees?"

"C'mon, I'm more creative than that. I broke the other leg falling off a horse when I was six. After that I had no intention of ever riding again."

"But you did?"

"The first day the doctor cleared me to ride Dad put me back in the saddle."

"Do you still ride?"

"Every time I come to the ranch. I just bought a new Appaloosa. I'll show him to you tomorrow."

"I'd like that. How did you break your leg the other time?"

"I fell out of the tree house while I was trying to nail up a no trespassing sign to keep Tague out."

She laughed.

"That sounded good," Durk said.

"What?"

"You. I'd forgotten what a nice laugh you have. Not stifled. Just open and natural, like you mean it."

"Thanks." So he did like something about her.

"I should warn you about my family before we go inside."

She gritted her teeth and waited. "Go on."

"They'll talk your ears off, sometimes all of them at once. They'll ask questions about our friendship, especially my mother. You don't have to answer them."

"How would I? I don't remember having ever met you before you showed up in my hospital room."

"Good answer."

"Will I like your mother?"

"If you don't, you'll be the first person I ever introduced to her that didn't. She'll love you."

Meghan adjusted her knit cap, keeping it at a jaunty angle. "Bruises, bandages, shaved head and all?"

"Even better. She's a champion of the underdog. Not that you're a dog," he teased, "but you do look as if you got the worst end of a bitch fight."

Meghan followed Durk up the steps to the wide, welcoming front porch with its display of fresh pumpkins and pots of blooming mums. It was a million times more inviting than the picture on the internet.

"Are you sure I've never been here before?"

"I'm positive. Why do you ask?"

"No reason." Except that she had the crazy feeling that she was coming home.

Chapter Twelve

The timing for dumping the body couldn't have been worse. Meghan Sinclair had left him no options. If she regained her memory and went to the local police with her allegations, they'd descend on his property like circling vultures. The basement would be the first place they looked.

If they descended the rickety stairs to his haven now they'd find nothing but empty paint cans, chipped two-by-fours, a gnarled rope, a toolbox and a wobbly stepladder. It would look just like every other basement in the area.

That wasn't the ultimate resolution but it would buy him time. He had to come up with a better plan. If not, he knew exactly what to do with the rope and the wobbly stepladder. It would take guts, but he had no doubts that he could do it.

He hoped it didn't come to that. He'd much prefer to silence Meghan. She was sucking up to

Durk Lambert now, but he wouldn't stay with a lowly P.I. for long. Men with his kind of money never did.

Her day would come. It was just a matter of time.

Chapter Thirteen

Durk stooped and kissed his mother on the cheek.

Her face lit up as if he'd handed her the moon. "It's good to have you home, son."

"It's good to be here." He put a hand on the small of Meghan's back. "This is Meghan Sinclair. Meghan, this is my mom, Carolina."

Carolina put out her hand and clasped Meghan's in more of a gesture of warmth than an actual handshake. "I'm so glad Durk brought you with him. He's told me some of what you've been going through, and it makes me shudder just to think about it. I hope being here will make it easier for you."

"I'm sure it will."

"Durk, why don't you take Meghan's bags to the guest room while I show her around the common areas so that she can make herself at home?"

"You got it, but don't wear her out with questions, Mom. She needs rest."

"No interrogation," Carolina promised. "Other than to ask what she'd like to drink."

"I'd love a glass of iced tea," Meghan said as she followed Carolina to the back of the house.

"I hope you like vegetable beef soup."

"Soup sounds terrific." And she was getting hungry now that her earlier bout with nausea had passed.

"Most of the vegetables were grown in our garden last summer and then frozen. And, of course, the beef is from Bent Pine cattle. It's the best beef money can buy. My sons Tague and Damien will point that out to you before you leave—several times."

"Durk told me that I worked a case for Tague and Alexis recently. He thinks I may have also met Damien and Emma briefly at the hunting camp where Damien, Alexis and her son were staying."

"You did. I told Alexis and Emma that you were coming, and they can't wait to see you. They're both out running errands this afternoon, but they'll be home soon."

"I'll try to get some rest before they arrive so I'll be decent company."

"You can meet the rest of the family later, as

well, but only when you're ready. We can be a bit overwhelming even for people who aren't recuperating."

Meghan stood at the end of a huge farmhouse kitchen table while Carolina filled three glasses with ice. Her first impression of the interior of the Lambert house was that it was the most welcoming and comfortable house she'd ever been in.

Her first impression of Carolina Lambert was that she was absolutely stunning. She walked with a grace that movie stars would have envied. Her smile lit up a room. Her style was simple, classic and impeccable. She was probably somewhere in her early fifties, but she was in great shape and had almost no wrinkles.

Her creased jeans were neither too loose nor too tight, but looked as if they'd been tailored personally for Carolina. Her white cotton shirt was tucked in at the waist and topped with a simple black leather belt. She wore stylish ankle boots and a pair of gold earrings. Her wedding ring set was also gold. The single diamond that adorned it was at least three carats.

But it was the effect she had on Meghan that made the biggest impact. They'd met only minutes ago, but already Meghan felt as if they were old friends.

Not that anyone could actually qualify as an old friend in her mind until the amnesia ran its course.

Carolina poured the tea from an antique cut glass pitcher. She set one of the glasses next to Meghan and proceeded to ladle soup that had been simmering on the range into two cobalt-colored bowls.

"Can I help with something?" Meghan asked.

"You can get two of the blue flowered napkins from that drawer just behind you, the one nearest the dishwasher."

Having a useful task to do made Meghan feel even more like a friend instead of a needy stray Durk had dragged home with him. She was sure that was Carolina's intention. The woman had Texas hospitality down to a fine art.

By the time Durk rejoined them, Meghan and Carolina had settled on a huge glassed-in porch with a view of the horse stables and beyond that the fenced pastures that seemed to stretch out endlessly.

"I hung your garment bag in the closet and I set the gray leather bag on the luggage rack for you to unpack after you've rested."

"Thank you."

Durk took the empty chair. "Now I'm starving. Let's eat."

And eat he did, with such relish that he was fun to watch. He finished off two bowls of soup and two large squares of cornbread slathered in butter. After that, he still had room for apple pie à la mode.

Meghan ate half a bowl of soup and half a square of cornbread. She was afraid to trust her stomach to more.

"I don't see how you eat like that and stay so thin," she said as Durk forked the last bite of his pie.

"I only eat like this when I'm at the ranch. Trust me, nowhere in the world do you get home cooking like this."

"It is delicious," Meghan agreed and turned to Carolina. "Do you do the cooking or do you have a chef?"

"I don't know if she qualifies as a chef, but Alda cooks breakfast and lunch during the week. Tague and Damien both keep ranchers' hours and since they get up with the sun, they're ready for their big meal about one. Most weekday evenings we have leftovers or a casserole that Alda prepares before she goes home around four."

"Mom shocked us all when she hired Alda to do the cooking," Durk said. "When I was growing up, she wouldn't let anyone near the range but her."

"But now I have grandchildren," Carolina said, "and a difficult time saying no to positions on the boards of my pet charitable organizations. But I get plenty of opportunity to cook on the weekends when we all kick in. Damien's grilling steaks tonight."

"Where is everybody now?" Durk asked.

"Your sisters-in-law and their little ones are running errands. Your grandmother retired to her bedroom after lunch to watch those old movies she loves so much, and your Aunt Sybil is napping."

"And the nurse?" Durk asked.

"She's around here somewhere. I'll send her to the guest room as soon as Meghan has finished lunch."

Meghan's relaxed mood vanished in a heartbeat. She glared at Durk. "You surely didn't hire a nurse for me?"

"You've suffered a concussion and you're still reeling from the effects."

"But you should have at least asked me first."

"I don't see why. I took responsibility for you when I brought you to the ranch. Besides, it's not a big deal."

It wasn't a big deal to him, but it was to her. It was... It was... It... She gave up trying to find excuses and faced the truth.

She was losing control of her life.

Not that it was Durk's fault, but she still didn't like to be treated as if she couldn't make decisions for herself.

Meghan pushed back from the table. "You're right, Durk. It's not a big deal. I'm sorry for sounding so ungrateful. It's just that I'm frustrated and tired."

Carolina set down her nearly empty glass and stood. "Why don't I show you to your room now, Meghan? And you should know that hiring the nurse isn't solely Durk's doing. I'd decided to hire a nurse even before I knew Durk was bringing you to the ranch."

And now even Carolina thought she was an unappreciative shrew. "It's okay," Meghan said. "You don't have to explain."

"I should if it helps ease the tension," Carolina insisted. "I don't know if Durk told you, but his aunt Sybil has pleurisy. It's not serious, but I have some other pressing responsibilities that require my time and attention this week and I wanted to make sure Sybil's recovery went smoothly."

Like mother, like son. Thoughtful and caring. And now Meghan really felt ungrateful for getting bent out of shape over the nurse. The Lamberts had welcomed her into their lives. Meghan was certain both Durk and Carolina were sorry they'd bothered.

"I'll walk Meghan to her room," Durk said. "We need to talk."

Carolina picked up their two bowls and Durk's pie saucer. "In that case, I'll just take care of these dishes."

"I could help," Meghan offered.

"Next time. You get some rest and we'll talk later."

Officially dismissed, Meghan followed Durk out of the kitchen and down a hallway. He walked ahead, his stride long and purposeful. The tension between them swelled.

He stopped, opened a door and ushered her inside. "This is your room for the duration. If it doesn't suit you, you can have mine and I'll sleep in here."

"I said I'm sorry, Durk. I can still go to a hotel. And I can pay for my own nurse."

He placed his hands on her shoulders and looked her square in the eyes. "Do you ever just give it up and give a guy a chance, Meghan?"

"You're the one who insisted I come here."

"And now I'm trying to figure out why."

Without warning, he pulled her into his arms and kissed her hard on the mouth. The kiss came as such a shock. She didn't have time to respond before he'd pulled away.

"Get some rest."

Her head was spinning as he turned and walked away. She didn't know what the kiss was about, but she did know that whatever passion they'd once shared hadn't all disappeared with the breakup.

She'd think about it later—when the imminent identification of a killer became more than a promise lost in the treacherous void that threatened to swallow her past.

"GOOD BREWSKI," Durk said. He took another gulp of the cold brew and hooked his heels around the bottom rung of the wooden fence that circled the corral.

"Nothing like a cold one after a fast ride," Tague agreed. He kicked a clump of mud from his boot before leaning against the fence post near where Damien and Durk had perched.

"I'll drink to that," Damien added. The brothers clinked bottles as a young mare started toward them and then skittishly galloped off to where some of the other horses were sticking their noses into a clump of fresh hay.

"I needed that ride almost as much as I needed this week at the ranch," Durk said. "It gets crazy in the oil business. Everybody knows what you should do, but they aren't the ones putting their heads in the noose if the project goes belly-up."

"Glad it's you holding those reins and not me," Tague said. "It's bad enough fighting the Washington bureaucrats who know nothing about ranching but spend their time sitting around dreaming up new regulations."

"So what's the deal with you and Meghan?" Tague asked, finally approaching the topic they'd all been talking around. "Are you two in a relationship or is this just a land and rescue operation?"

"It's an act of friendship. Meghan's having a rough go of it. Not only is she bruised and battered, but losing her memory and having her assistant murdered have left her in a seriously vulnerable position. Once I realized that, I could hardly just walk away."

"Doesn't she have family?" Tague asked.

"A married sister in Connecticut. But Lucy's out of commission herself. She's eight months pregnant and the doctor has ordered total bed rest."

"Tough luck," Damien said. "I guess Meghan doesn't remember her sister, either."

"No, and she hasn't even talked with her by

phone yet. I've been keeping Lucy and her husband up-to-date on Meghan's condition."

"Why doesn't Meghan talk to her?" Tague asked.

"I think she's afraid that if she talks to Lucy and it doesn't jog her memory then nothing else will. She's not ready to face that."

"I'm not up on amnesia," Damien admitted, "but I wouldn't think Meghan could lose her memory permanently if there's no measurable brain damage."

"From what I've researched on the internet and what Dr. Levy said, that would be extremely rare, unless there are extenuating emotional issues at play. But she may go months or forever without remembering events immediately surrounding the attack."

Damien finished his beer and placed the empty bottle on the ground at his feet. "So what you're saying is that even when she regains her memory, she may not be able to identify the man who attacked her and likely killed her assistant."

"That's about the size of it. In the meantime, the killer is still out there. But we have had some developments that could be helpful. I know I don't need to tell you that what I'm about to share should stay between us for now."

"However you want it handled, bro." Damien spoke for his brother.

Durk explained the message Detective Smart had replayed for them, the visit from Meghan's "brother" and the chat they'd had with Connie Latimer.

"So you think Meghan could still be in danger?" Damien asked.

"Not on the ranch with all three of us and twenty or more wranglers armed for rattlers around. He's not going to risk getting shot after all the trouble he's gone to in order to cover his tracks."

"What you're saying is the bastard doesn't mind killing, as long as he's not the one who ends up dead."

"Exactly. I figure he'll bide his time—unless he's pushed into a corner. No reason to think he's there yet."

"So the plan is just to sit and wait until Meghan remembers him or the details of the cases she was working or until the police make an arrest?" Damien asked.

"You know me better than that. Meghan Sinclair is one of the best private investigators in the business when it comes to tracking down criminals the cops couldn't catch, but there are a few others who are just as good or better scattered around the globe."

"Best not let Meghan hear you say that." Damien said.

"Not a chance," Durk said.

"So who are these P.I. prospects?" Tague asked.

"There's a former Interpol agent living in Europe now whose reputation is stellar. In fact, he's so good, the French are making a movie based on his life. And there's a former FBI forensics expert who's fast becoming the go-to P.I. on this continent. I have calls in to both of them."

"Might as well go with the best," Tague said.

"I also have this." Durk reached into his shirt pocket and pulled out a folded copy of the multipage printout of phone calls made to and from Meghan's cell and office phones for the prior month. He handed the list to Tague, who scanned it and passed it on to Damien.

"That's a lot of phone calls," Damien said. "Meghan could probably make short work of it if she could remember these calls, but it could take you days to check all those out and see which ones could be suspect."

"I can help," Tague said.

"Count me in, too," Damien said. "Though I've got a full day scheduled on Monday."

"I've already faxed a copy of this to Jackson Phelps," Durk said. Phelps was former NCIS and now a P.I. who did some work for Durk's company. "He's going to cross-reference the numbers with names and addresses and see which ones are likely business related, such as other P.I.s or police connections, as well as her personal calls like hair and nail appointments and her local pizza delivery."

"Or a boyfriend," Damien said. "Is there any reason to think she isn't seeing anyone?"

"No reason at all," Durk admitted. "If we locate a boyfriend, maybe he'll know something that could help." He hoped he sounded a lot more unaffected by the idea of a boyfriend than he felt.

Falling for Meghan again was not part of his plan, but she was definitely getting to him. He could barely keep his hands off her. And now he'd kissed her. He couldn't let that happen again.

"Good choice in pulling Jackson in on this," Tague said. "He did a hell of a job keeping Alexis and Tommy safe. Now what's this big day you have planned on Monday, Damien? It's not on the headquarters calendar."

Damien stuffed his hands into the front pockets of his jeans. "I had a call from the P.I. I hired to find Belle's father."

There was no missing the torment in Damien's voice.

"Has he found a lead?"

"He thinks he may have found the man. Juan Perez. He came from the same little village in Mexico as Belle's mother."

"I didn't know you had that information on Belle's mother."

"The P.I. was able to track it down. Anyway, Juan lives in Galveston and works for one of the hotels on the beach. He's married. No kids. No criminal record. And he's legal. If Belle's his daughter, there would be nothing to keep him from claiming her."

Tague clapped Damien on the shoulder. "Oh, man, that's a shocker. After all these months, and with you and Emma growing even more attached to Belle. And Mom. She's crazy about that baby. Hell, we all are."

"How's Emma taking this?" Durk asked.

"I haven't told her."

"Don't you think you should?"

"Yeah, but I can't bring myself to do it unless I know for certain we're going to lose her. Emma's taken care of Belle ever since she took the infant from her dying mother's arms. Belle probably wouldn't even be alive if it weren't for Emma's bravery."

"Will you have any rights as foster parents? After all, if Emma hadn't been escaping a demented kidnapper, Belle would have likely been tossed from the human trafficking van with her dead mother."

Damien shrugged. "We have the right to a broken heart. But we knew this could happen going in. We took the risk. You can never go wrong by choosing love. That's been Emma's motto all along."

It was a nice motto, but Durk wasn't convinced it was true. He knew there were no guarantees in life, but if he chose love, he'd at least want the odds in his favor. He was smart enough to know that would never be the case with a P.I. who'd go to any extreme to solve a case.

"One more beer?" Tague asked.

"Not for me," Damien said. "I want to spend some time with Belle before I start grilling the steaks."

"I need to get back to the house, too," Durk said. "Meghan's probably awake by now, and I should make sure she's feeling okay."

Tague smirked. "The Lambert brothers and the women and children who claim their hearts and rule their lives. Things are changing around the whole home place, John Boy."

"Speak for yourselves," Durk said. "I'm still totally my own man."

Tague gave him a playful punch on the arm. "And that's what's known as denial."

They walked back to the house together as the sun began a fast descent, painting the clouds in beautiful streaks of color. There was nothing like the bonds that tied him to his brothers. He hated to think of ever having to handle real trouble without knowing they were on his side.

The bond between sisters had to be just as close. It might even work miracles where memories were concerned. At least it was worth a shot.

This time he wouldn't give Meghan a chance to say no. It might backfire on him, but then he'd been known to wade into a bar fight with a smile on his face before.

Chapter Fourteen

The sun was setting by the time Meghan woke from her nap. She didn't even remember undressing, but her jeans and sweater were neatly draped over a chair near the window and she was only wearing her panties and bra.

She stretched beneath the cool sheets and took her first good look around what Durk had referred to as the first-floor guest suite. It was in the west wing of the house, and from her bed she had a view of the pool and a charming garden.

A gorgeous fall arrangement graced the heavy wooden table that sat next to an intricately detailed rocker. A flowery fragrance filled the air.

The mattress was like floating on a cloud, especially compared to the bed at the hospital, which was the only bed she remembered.

But no matter how tempting the bed, she'd best get up and put some clothes on before Durk or another Lambert came to check on her. She stretched one last time and walked over to the en suite bathroom, a charming space with an antique claw-foot tub and a dressing table that reminded her of a European boudoir.

The mix of furnishings was eclectic, but it all seemed to fit with the feel of the house. She suspected that was due to Carolina's sense of timeless style.

As much as she liked Carolina, Meghan dreaded their next encounter. She hated that she'd made such a scene over the nurse, but there was nothing she could do about that now. The nurse must have heard about it, as well. If she'd checked on Meghan at all, it had been while she was napping. But then she had slept most of the afternoon.

Meghan washed her hands and face and then studied the stranger in the mirror. Her face was still bruised on one side, but the hematoma had reduced, making her not quite as lopsided.

She finger combed her hair back in place. It framed her face well and fell nicely over her shoulders. The problem area was the back of her head. Reluctantly, Meghan picked up a handheld mirror from the dressing table for a better look.

The bandage would have been fine. It was the area of shaved head around the bandage that made it look as if she'd been scalped.

But as bad as she looked and as badly as she'd behaved, Durk had kissed her, albeit roughly, almost as if it were bitter medicine he was forced to swallow.

So why couldn't she get the quick, meaningless kiss off her mind? Worse, she wanted him to kiss her again. She didn't know if it was her vulnerability or some unremembered remnant of past passion, but she couldn't deny the attraction she had for him.

Even if he felt the same, it was the wrong place and the wrong time to act on an attraction that she'd apparently sampled and rejected in the past.

A tap on her door jerked her from the traitorous thoughts.

"Just a minute." She hurriedly put on her clothes.

"If you're resting we can come back later."

Once again, she didn't recognize the voice.

"I'm not resting and I'd love company. So please don't go." Loving company was a bit of exaggeration. What she would love was to visit with someone she could actually remember.

She opened the door to two very attractive women who were somewhere near her age, a rambunctious toddler with mischievous eyes and an adorable baby girl who was trying her best to wiggle from her mother's arms.

"I'm Alexis," the shapely blonde announced as she pulled Meghan into a warm hug. "I know you don't remember me yet, but we hit it off when we met a few months back. And this is Emma."

"We've met, as well," Emma said. "I'm really sorry to hear about the problems you're facing. I know this is a bad time for you."

"Thanks. I'm just taking things one day at a time. It's all I can do."

The boy ran to the window and pointed at the pool. "We go swim, Mommy."

"I'm sorry, sweetie. It's too cold for swimming today."

"Not too cold," he argued. "Go get Daddy."

"Your daddy is not taking you swimming, either. He's working."

The boy stamped his foot once then promptly ran off to check out a colorful paperweight on the corner of a small desk.

"And now you've met Tommy," Alexis said.

"He's delightful. How old is he?"

"He just turned three, and if he gets any more active, I'm going to have to wear skates to keep up with him."

"And this is Belle," Emma said, holding her

up for Alexis to get a better look. "She's nine months old."

"Hello, Belle. You are a cutie pie."

Belle babbled and clapped her hands as if she understood the compliment.

"We don't want to tire you," Emma said, "but we had to stop in and say hello."

"And we come bearing welcome gifts," Alexis added.

"You didn't need to do that."

"It's not much. It's not easy shopping with Tommy and Belle reaching for everything you pass."

But Alexis was smiling as she reached into a reusable shopping bag and pulled out a box of chocolates, some mints and a ribbon-bedecked jar of bath oil beads.

"You are so thoughtful. I can't wait to sink into a relaxing bath."

"We thought about buying you a paperback," Emma said, "but we don't know what you'd read or what kind of novels you like to read."

"Nor do I," Meghan said. "How weird is that?"

"I can't even imagine," Emma said. "So I thought you might want this." She handed Meghan an iPad. "That's not a gift, but you're welcome to use it as long as you're here."

"I will. I used Durk's while I was in the hospital. I looked him and myself up on Google. I even found a picture of the Lambert house online, but I think it was heavily altered."

"I bet I know which picture you mean," Alexis said. "It was in some kind of women's magazine. Carolina said the photographer was so disappointed when he showed up that he had props brought in. He received the ultimate Lambert insult for that."

"What would that be?"

"He was not invited to stay for dinner."

Meghan laughed along with Emma and Alexis.

"It was really lucky Durk had stopped by the hospital to see Sybil the night you were attacked," Alexis said. "He's such a terrific guy. All three of the Lambert men are."

"They take protection to whole new levels," Emma said. "Belle and I both owe our lives to Damien."

"Same here. Tague put his life on the line for me," Alexis said. "And the Lambert men do it as naturally as if they were helping you mount a horse."

"Durk has been great," Meghan admitted. "But I won't be here long, and hopefully I won't need the kind of protection you did. The doctor just wasn't keen on releasing me from the hospital while I was still having headaches and occasional dizzy spells. Durk was gracious enough to invite me to the ranch so that I wouldn't be home alone."

"How are the headaches?" Emma asked.

"Much better," she lied. "Especially since you dropped in to cheer me up. And I'm not dizzy at all, at least not at this minute."

"You'll get great care while you're here. The Lambert women are masters of TLC, especially Carolina," Emma assured her.

"And the Lambert men are all extremely handsome," Alexis said, adding a little physical dramatics to the statement.

"I can't remember your husbands," Meghan said. "But Durk is nice-looking."

"And you're blushing talking about him," Alexis said. "I knew there was something more than just business between you and Durk the first time his name came up in conversation when you were working with Tague and me."

"Then you know more than I do. Durk is as much a stranger to me at the moment as everyone else in my life."

"You liked him. That was obvious. But you two were on the outs."

Meghan would love to hear more, but she

didn't dare pursue the conversation for risk of letting Alexis and Emma know how attracted she was to Durk. "I can't even think about a romance until my memory returns."

"Romance doesn't consider convenience or timelines," Alexis said. "And it can't be scripted. It happens when you least expect it, at least it did for Tague and me."

"I'll keep that in mind."

There was another tap on the door. This time it was the nurse.

"I just wanted to check your blood pressure and see if your bandage needs changing. But I can come back when your guests leave."

"No. We've bothered Meghan enough," Emma said. "The patient is all yours."

Belle started waving. "Bye-bye. Bye-bye."

"Bye-bye, Belle."

Tommy grabbed Belle's waving hand and put it on his head. She giggled appropriately at his antics.

"Oh, by the way," Meghan asked, "what's the dress code for dinner?"

"There's never an official dress code unless it's a party. We'll definitely be wearing jeans tonight. Damien's grilling steaks and Tague is doing his famous campfire potatoes," Emma explained. "They're both so excited about having Durk home that it will likely turn into one of those male bonding nights. But the food will be great. It always is."

"See you at dinner," Alexis added as she closed the door behind them.

The nurse introduced herself as she fit the blood pressure cuff around Meghan's arm.

"Aren't the Lamberts just the nicest family?" she asked. "They're not snooty at all."

"Not at all," Meghan agreed.

Durk Lambert had been blessed with solid roots and good genes. He'd likely make a great husband and father one day.

Meghan was far less sure of her qualifications for a wife and mother. The amnesia had made her a stranger to herself. But Durk had known her as a lover. He'd obviously not been impressed.

And yet he'd welcomed her right back into his life. He was a hard man to figure. She suspected he'd be even harder to forget.

MEGHAN KICKED OUT of her shoes and pulled her feet into the chair with her while she checked out every Google reference to herself that she could find. There were hundreds. Apparently she'd gotten around, working cases from the East Coast to the West Coast.

She'd gained a bit of notoriety in New York last year when one of the cases she'd investigated solved the murders of two coeds from different schools who'd disappeared from the same jogging trail exactly one month apart. She'd cornered their killer herself and almost gotten killed in the process.

She'd been quoted as saying that, in hindsight, it was not a smart move. No kidding.

Had she made a similar mistake this time? Had it cost Ben Conroe his life? If so, she'd have to live with his blood on her hands for the rest of her life. But she wouldn't stop until the killer was apprehended.

She turned off the digital tablet. She'd learned enough about herself for one afternoon. It was almost six. She should go down and see if there was something she could do to help with dinner. Hopefully, Carolina had written off her rudeness as a side effect of the concussion.

Meghan had just slipped into a pair of comfortable boots when she heard footsteps and a firm tap on the door.

"Come in."

Durk stepped inside. "Good. You're awake."

"What's up?"

He held out his cell phone. "You have a call."

If someone was calling her on his phone, it was likely Detective Smart or Dr. Levy.

She put it to her ear. "Hello."

"Meghan. How are you?"

The voice burst inside Meghan's head like a balloon, releasing shiny slivers of colored jewels that fluttered through her mind.

She struggled for breath. "Lucy?"

"Yes. And you recognized my voice."

"I did. Oh, my God, Lucy." Tears wet her eyes and emotion clogged her throat. "I'm so glad you called."

"Me, too. Durk didn't think you even remembered me."

"I don't. I mean, I didn't. But now I do. It's like someone raised a blind and let the sunshine back into my mind. Do I sound crazy?"

"Not at all. You sound great. I've been so worried about you."

"I was attacked in my condo."

"I know. Durk told me everything. He's been great at keeping Johnny and me up to date on everything."

"Who's Johnny?"

"Johnny—my husband. We were married three years ago. You were my maid of honor."

"Oh, gee. I'm picturing you as twelve years old. But you can't be. You're my age."

"I'm two years older than you, but who's counting?"

"I remember when you thought being the oldest was a badge of honor."

"It meant I got to drive and date sooner."

"I don't remember you driving a car. But I remember that year we both got new bikes and you dented yours the first day and then tried to bribe me to trade with you."

"That was a very long time ago. Do you remember being in my wedding?"

Meghan tried to picture Lucy in a wedding dress. The image wouldn't jell. The Lucy bobbing around in her thoughts had a ponytail and skinned knees.

Apprehension swelled again. "I can't remember your wedding, Lucy."

"Don't worry. You will soon. What do you remember?"

"Us as kids. And Mother. I remember Mother."

"That's great."

"Not all of it is great. I'm picturing Mother the day she told us Daddy was killed in the war. I remember how she cried and couldn't stop. I remember it like it was yesterday."

And now Meghan was crying. She sniffled and reached for a tissue from the box on her bedside table.

"Your nose is going to light up like Rudolph's if you don't stop crying, Meghan."

"I know. But the tears are partly out of happiness. I actually remember things from my past."

"Durk said that your neurologist had told you that you had *temporary* retrograde amnesia.

"I know, but it's a frightening feeling to wake up and have no memory of who you are or where you are or how you got there. And there's no specific timeline of 'temporary.'"

"I know. I was afraid for you. I wanted to catch the first plane to Dallas, but I'm pregnant."

"You're pregnant? Did I know that?"

"You did. I'm eight months pregnant. You're going to have a niece."

"Then I'm flying up to see you—wherever you live."

"Connecticut. Are you still having headaches?"

"The headaches come and go, but they're not nearly as painful and annoying as they were. I still get dizzy at times. I'm a little light-headed now, but I think that could be from pure relief and the excitement of talking to you."

Meghan looked up. Durk was not around. He'd slipped away without her noticing. She owed him big-time for making her take this call.

"What's your most recent memory?" Lucy asked.

Meghan let her head fall back to the pillow as she tried to remember her life as an adult. She hit a brick wall. "I seem to be lost in a time warp. I don't remember high school or college. Dr. Levy warned me that I might recover memories in bits and pieces."

"And apparently you are."

"I can live with that, now that I realize the memories are just trapped in a fog. I have a sister again, one I actually remember. How long has it been since I told you that I love you?"

"Too long. I miss you and love you, too, sweetie. I wish I could be there with you, but you seem to be making it fine without me. Being taken care of by Durk Lambert. Living the life of the rich and famous. You, sister, have it made."

"So it would seem."

"Tell me again why you two broke up."

"You'll have to wait for the sequel for that information. Return of the Memories Part Two."

"I can't wait. Can I call you every day now that you're speaking to me again?"

"Please do. You'll have to call me on Durk's phone, though. Mine is no longer in service. Nor is my computer, not that I remember any of my passwords. And my car is gone. All thanks to a madman who is still on the loose."

"You have your life, Meghan. That's what really counts."

"But my assistant doesn't. I guess Durk told you that."

"He told Johnny, and Johnny finally told me everything, at least I think he has. He's as protective as your Durk."

"Durk doesn't belong to me, but he is protective. I'm still not sure why."

"He's crazy about you."

"Sure. I bet that's why we broke up." She'd talked enough about Durk. "Did I happen to tell you anything about the case I was working on before the attack?"

"No. You never tell me about your cases. I wouldn't let you if you wanted to. I worry about you enough as it is."

"You're sure I didn't mention any names or places?"

"Meghan, please promise me you're not getting involved in Ben's murder investigation."

But Meghan wouldn't make a promise she couldn't keep. "I have to go now. I'm having dinner with the Lamberts. I'll talk to you tomorrow."

"Stay safe, Meghan. For once, don't make this

your personal vendetta. Let the cops do their job. All you need to do is get better and stay safe."

"I have every intention of doing both of those. Talk later. Love you."

Meghan broke the connection and walked to the bathroom to douse her eyes with cold water. She was standing at the sink when the vertigo hit again. She held on to the basin for support until she was steady enough to stagger back to the bed.

CAROLINA STOOD AT the counter, peeling the skin from the fresh-dug yams her cantankerous neighbor R. J. Dalton had dropped off that afternoon. She hadn't planned on baking tonight, but the phone call she'd just received from Mary Nell Conroe was troubling. And nothing calmed Carolina the way baking did.

Durk walked into the kitchen, poured himself a cup of coffee and joined her at the counter. "Need some help?"

"Sure." She handed him the peeler she'd been using and grabbed another one from the drawer.

"Candied sweet potatoes less than a week before Thanksgiving? Aren't you afraid that will take away from the big day?"

"It would. I'm making pies with these."

"Sweet potato pies. My favorite."

"You say that about every pie I make."

"And I'm always telling the truth."

"I hope Meghan likes them."

"If she doesn't, I'll eat her share. But you shouldn't count on her for dinner or dessert."

"Why not? She's not still upset that I hired a nurse, is she?"

"Don't fault her for that, Mother. She's under a lot of stress."

"I realize that. Is she feeling okay now?"

"I just went in to check on her and get my phone back and she was sound asleep. She didn't get much sleep in the hospital last night so I'm not going to wake her. But the good news is that she talked to her sister and she recognized Lucy's voice."

"Oh, my. That is good news."

"But don't question her about it," Durk cautioned. "She's trying to come to grips with a lot of things right now, and I don't know how much she remembers."

"I won't question her about anything."

"That's probably the best policy for now."

Carolina reached around Durk for another potato. "I haven't had a chance to tell you, but Mary Nell Conroe called me this afternoon."

"And I haven't had a chance to tell you how

much I appreciate your help in getting rid of her yesterday."

"I was glad to help. She needed someone to talk to."

"Why did she call today?"

"To tell me that Ben's funeral will be on Tuesday. She thought I might know how to get in touch with Meghan in case she wanted to attend."

"I hope that means she's no longer blaming Meghan for Ben's death."

"All I know is that she seemed to want Meghan at the funeral."

"I'm not sure that's a good idea."

"Shouldn't you let Meghan decide that? He was her friend and a coworker."

"I don't know if she even remembers him yet. Just because she recognized Lucy's voice doesn't mean the amnesia has evaporated."

"She'll eventually remember him. When she does, she might need the degree of closure a funeral offers."

"What she needs is for the police to make an arrest."

"That could take months."

"Or years. Or never. I don't plan to let that happen."

"Stay out of crime solving, Durk. You have

enough on your plate without trying to do the DPD's work for them."

"You didn't tell that to Damien or Tague when they put their lives on the line for Emma and Alexis."

"That was different."

"How was it different?"

"Emma and Alexis didn't ask for the trouble they were in. They weren't private investigators. They're not out purposefully looking for danger again and again."

"What makes you think Meghan does that?"

"I checked her out after talking to Mary Nell. She has a reputation for tracking down killers like the one who killed Ben. I don't want you jumping into danger just because she does."

"I'm sorry you feel that way, Mother. But I won't turn my back on Meghan as long as she's in danger. You and Dad taught me to be a bigger man than that."

Durk dropped the half-peeled potato into the sink and walked out. She'd probably handled this all wrong.

"Oh, Hugh, I miss you so much. If you were here, you'd know what to say to Durk."

Tague stepped behind her and put his hands on her shoulders.

"I didn't hear you come in." She kept peeling without turning around.

"I know those whispered words weren't for me, Mom. But I think I can tell you what Dad would say. He'd tell you a man has to do what he thinks is right or he isn't a real man. Durk's a real man, Mom."

She caught an escaping tear with the corner of her apron. "Well, I can at least pray for him."

"We all can." Tague kissed the top of her head and walked away.

Her sons had all grown to be men. They were no longer hers to teach and guide and make certain they were safe. She would always be their mother, but now they belonged to the women in their lives.

Durk belonged to Meghan. He hadn't accepted that as certainty yet, but Carolina had a sixth sense about these things. He wasn't as quick as Damien and Tague to go where angels feared to tread.

Hugh always said that Durk was the wary one. He checked things out first. Tested the waters. Then he went right ahead and did whatever it was he'd been worrying about. And he did it with gusto.

They'd made more trips to the emergency room with him than the other two boys together.

But Durk was different with Meghan than she'd ever seen him with a woman. He was still in the wary stage, but when he jumped it would be with both feet and no holds barred. And it would be forever.

Meghan had a taste for danger that was yet to be quenched. Durk had a sense of loyalty that would never be dissolved.

Carolina had plenty of reason to worry.

MEGHAN JUMPED IN her sleep and woke abruptly from a deep, trancelike state. She'd been so out of it that for a second she thought she might have slept through the night.

She rolled over and looked at the clock. Five minutes past nine.

Not nearly as late as she'd feared, but she'd surely missed dinner. Not that she was particularly hungry, but she didn't want to appear rude after her lunchtime performance.

She was still fully dressed. Perhaps it wasn't too late to join the Lamberts for dessert. She slid from the bed and walked over to check her appearance in the full-length mirror behind the bathroom door.

The jeans were fine. The sweater was rumpled. Meghan pulled it over her head, tossed it back into the closet and chose a pale green shirt that wouldn't clash with her purplish bruises. A quick smoothing of her hair and a touch of lip gloss and she was as good as she was going to get tonight.

The house was quiet as she made her way to the kitchen. The male bonding had either ended early or the men were outside. Emma and Alexis were probably putting their little ones to bed, unless they'd done that before dinner.

Meghan would have expected that with the wealth the Lamberts had accumulated, both Emma and Alexis would have nannies caring for their children. Instead they seemed to enjoy taking care of them themselves. If Meghan ever had children, she'd like to be like these women.

It was odd not to know if she'd ever thought about having children or could have them if she wanted to. Clearly, the Lamberts were family oriented. The ranch was almost like a commune with so many people in one house. And she had yet to meet Durk's aunt Sybil or his grandma Pearl.

She started to turn back when she realized the lights were out in the kitchen. Then she decided to get a glass of water while she was up.

The shadowed figure standing at the back door startled her until she realized it was Durk. Even from the back, he was incredibly handsome. His shoulders were broad, his body hard and lean.

She fought the impulse to walk over to him and fit herself into his arms. It would be a daring move.

But they had been lovers once. She imagined his naked body pressed against hers. Imagined his lips kissing her senseless before exploring her body inch by torrid inch.

Now she was carrying things too far. She cleared her throat so that he'd turn around before she fantasized herself right into his arms.

He spun around. "I didn't hear you walk up, but I'm glad you did. I was just debating whether I should let you sleep or warm you a plate of leftovers and serve you in bed."

Being served in bed would have been very romantic, especially if he'd snacked with her. She was pretty sure he wasn't thinking that way. "I'm sorry I missed having dinner with your family. I hadn't planned to fall asleep again. I just drifted off without warning."

"You're here to sleep and relax and not have to worry about schedules. Besides, I figured the emotional impact of talking to Lucy wore you out."

"I was so engrossed in the moment, I didn't see you leave. I was hoping you stuck around long enough to realize that I recognized Lucy's voice."

"Absolutely. I wouldn't have missed that. But then I left so that you two could have some privacy."

"Thanks for making that happen in spite of my protests."

"You're welcome. What's the status on your memory now?"

"I still have quite a way to go, but at least it was a step in the right direction. Mostly it was childhood memories that came back to me. Unfortunately, I still don't remember anything about the case I was working for Connie Latimer so I still can't be certain that it was related to Ben's murder."

"Then I assume you don't remember the actual attack?"

"I'm still drawing a complete blank there, too. I hate that I can't get a handle on things."

"It'll happen. Just give it time. Now how about some food? I saved you a steak and some potatoes. Or if you'd like something light, Mom always has yogurt and fruit in the fridge."

"The yogurt sounds good."

"I'll get you a spoon," Durk said. "You can check the supply and pick out the flavor you want."

Meghan opened the refrigerator and leaned over to search the laden shelves.

"Scoot stuff out of the way if you need to," Durk said. He came over to help.

Their hands met in the refrigerator. Hers tangled with his. His tangled with a jar of strawberry preserves. They caught the jar together before it tumbled to the tile floor.

Their laugher intermingled. A split second later Durk's arms were around her and Meghan reeled from the mesmerizing sensation of being exactly where she belonged.

Chapter Fifteen

Durk reacted instantaneously, his desire turning rock hard. The hunger for Meghan was fast pushing him over the edge. But if he kissed her, he might never be able to stop. Making out with Meghan right here in the kitchen where someone in his family might walk in on them at any second was out of the question.

Hell. What was he thinking? He shouldn't even have his arms around her. She wasn't just emotionally vulnerable; she was recovering from a concussion. She'd checked out of the hospital today against the doctor's recommendation. He was supposed to be watching over her.

Durk let his arms drop from around her and stepped away. He had to keep a clear head. "Do you feel like taking a walk?"

"If that's what you want."

"It's what I need. There are some light jackets

hanging in the laundry room. Wait here, and I'll get us a couple."

He breathed easier when he had walked away from her, but the desire was still riding him hard. He'd thought he was making progress in getting over her. The reaction he'd just had proved he was as bewitched as ever.

He should have hired all the help she needed, but he should have never brought her to the Bent Pine. But she was here now. He had to get his act together.

Once they'd stepped onto the back porch, he helped her into the jacket. He had a flashlight in the pocket of his, but there was little chance he'd need it. The moon was almost full and sparkling stars filled the sky. As if he needed a romantic backdrop tonight.

"It's beautiful out here," she said as they descended the steps. "The stars look as if I could reach up and grab one."

"I think about that sometimes when I'm away on a business trip to the other side of the world," Durk said. "Well, not actually about touching the stars but how the same stars that I see here seem just as near when I'm continents away, yet the Bent Pine Ranch seems light-years away."

"Do you travel a lot?"

"I have lately. It's the nature of the oil business

and our shrinking world. It's always good to get back to Texas, though, and especially great to get back to the ranch."

"Yet you chose to go into the oil business while your brothers chose the ranching lifestyle."

"Many things about the corporate world appeal to me."

"For instance?"

"The responsibility. The challenges. The constant technological innovation. The interaction with all kinds of people from all over the world.

"Besides, it's a family business. My grandfather and his father built it up from scratch when oil was first discovered on the land. I've always thought Lambert Inc. should have a Lambert at the helm."

Durk started to relax. As long as they kept walking and stuck to safe topics, he could handle this.

"But you really are a cowboy at heart," Meghan said. "I didn't quite buy the cowboy clothes and easy mannerisms once I realized you were a wealthy entrepreneur, but seeing you on the ranch and interacting with your family, I get it."

"See? I'm not that complicated once you get to know me."

"How well did I get to know you when we were dating?"

"I couldn't say. We didn't do a lot of talking those first few weeks. We were too consumed with the physical side of the relationship. But I'm pretty much what you see is what you get."

"Yet you admitted that you never brought me to the Bent Pine. Was that because I didn't want to come or you didn't think I'd fit in?"

Somehow he'd let the conversation take a bad turn. He wouldn't lie to her, but there was no use getting into painful truths tonight. "It's been two years since we dated, Meghan. Are you sure you want to get back into all of that again?"

She grabbed his hand and tugged him to a stop. "Kiss me, Durk. Not the way you did this afternoon, but the way you did when we first met."

"I don't think that's a good idea."

"Then stop thinking and just lead with your mouth."

He should run like hell from this kind of temptation. But when she put her arms around him and pulled his mouth to hers, he gave up the fight. He took Meghan in his arms and pressed his hungry lips against hers.

She melted into the kiss, yielding at first and then giving way to passion with the same wild, uninhibited fervor she always had before. Holding nothing back, as ravenous for him as he was for her, she toyed and nipped and sucked and parried until the thrill of her drove him absolutely crazy with desire.

Blood rushed to his head, the need for her so explosive he could feel it deep inside his soul.

But this was not what she needed. Not now. Not this soon after the attack. He forced himself to step away from her. "We should go back inside while I can still walk."

"Not yet."

"Meghan, I'm trying to do what's right, but I have only so much control."

"I won't push myself on you again. But there's something I have to know."

"Shoot."

"You said we split because we didn't work together. I thought you meant there had been no magic. I know better now. What we just shared is dynamite."

"It was always dynamite with you."

"So why did we break up?"

It wasn't the time or the place for this discussion, but he could tell Meghan was not going to drop it until he gave her an honest answer.

She shoved her hands in the jacket pockets. "Was there someone else?"

"Don't ever think that. I couldn't get enough of you. I went to work and counted the hours until I could see you again. I canceled business trips or sent someone else in my place because I didn't want to spend a night without you in my arms."

"But I simply wasn't the one you wanted to take home to meet the family."

"That's not how it was, not even close."

"Then what was it? My job." Her hands flew to her hips. "It was my job, wasn't it? Billionaire CEOs do not marry private investigators. I would have embarrassed you, out chasing killers when the other wives were shopping for their designer clothes and throwing debutante parties."

Her accusations were as frustrating as everything else about this night. He threw up his hands in exasperation.

"If you think I'm so shallow and superficial that I'd give a rat's behind about whether or not you shopped for designer clothes and hobnobbed with a bunch of socialites, then you don't know me at all, Meghan."

"That's just it. I don't know you, Durk. You have memories of us. I just have this inexplicable attraction and all the mixed signals you keep giving out. All I'm asking for is a level playing field."

"What mixed signals do you think I'm giving out?"

"You put your life on hold to take care of me when we haven't even exchanged a phone call in two years. You bring me home and insinuate me into your family when you'd never even introduced me to them while we were supposedly in a hot-and-heavy relationship."

"Okay, Meghan. You made your point. You want the truth? I'll give it to you. It *was* your job that broke us up. Not because there's anything wrong with your profession. The problem was with the way you do your job."

"What the devil is that supposed to mean?"

"You deliberately blur the lines between what you do and what should be left to law enforcement. You take unnecessary risks and put yourself in danger over and over and over again."

"We could have talked about it before you just blew me off."

"No, we couldn't—because you didn't want to talk about it. You were at the top of your game and your profession and you made it clear you had no intention of changing. And I didn't blow you off. You broke up with me because you said I wanted more than you could give. I couldn't argue with that."

"Then maybe you did want too much. I don't

remember the past, Durk, but I know that I'll do whatever it takes to make sure the no-good murderous monster who killed Ben Conroe will pay for the crime. If that means I'm not the kind of woman you want in your life, then you're probably not man enough for me anyway."

"That goes without saying. I'm not man enough to leave you every morning and worry that you're meeting a murderer for lunch. I can't plan a life with you only to come home one night and realize that I'll never hold you in my arms again because you took one risk too many instead of handing the information over to the police."

"Then you were right, Durk. It really was over for us before it ever got started. I'm cold and ready to go back inside now."

Durk was cold, too, all the way down to his soul. He expected to feel that way for a long, long time.

MEGHAN HAD PUSHED the issue. She'd demanded answers and now she had to live with them.

The kitchen lights were on and she could hear laughter as they approached the house. Evidently, everyone had not been in bed earlier but had merely gone back to their private quarters.

Now at least some of the Lamberts had reassembled and she'd have to walk right past them.

She'd have to speak to them and pretend that she hadn't just sabotaged any future she might have had with Durk. Magic was not enough. Love didn't solve every problem the way they promised in movies, books and songs.

Durk took her arm as they climbed the steps, no doubt making sure she was steady and that her verbal outburst hadn't caused a surge of vertigo.

That was Durk. Protective of her in spite of the tension that dogged their every step.

They entered through the laundry room and hung their jackets on metal hooks next to the door.

"Hey, just in time for pie and hot chocolate," Alexis called before they'd even reached the kitchen door. "We wondered where you two had gone off to."

Meghan felt as if the air was being sucked from her lungs as they joined the two couples in the cozy kitchen. Tague was pouring hot chocolate into tall white mugs. Damien was serving pie. Emma and Alexis were sitting at the table, dressed in their pajamas, faces scrubbed clean of makeup.

Damien held up an empty pie-serving wedge. "Who's in for pie? There's two slices left."

Meghan's stomach rolled, a warning of what it would do if she pushed food into it. "None for me," she said. "I'm a bit nauseous tonight."

"In that case, I *almost* forgive you for missing out on my perfect steaks," Damien said.

"I can fix you a scrambled egg if that would sit better on your stomach," Emma offered.

"No, really, nothing for me. I hate to be a party pooper, but I'm feeling a little tired. If you'll excuse me, I think I'll retire to the guest quarters."

"You do look a little shaky," Alexis said. "Where's your pager? You should alert the nurse."

"The pager is next to my bed, and I promise I will use it if I need to."

"I think you're supposed to keep the pager with you at all times," Emma cautioned. "That way you can let her know if you get dizzy or feel faint."

"I think our walk just wore her out," Durk said. "But I'll see that the nurse checks on her."

Durk didn't look up as Meghan walked away. He joined in the animated camaraderie with his family while she was left to deal with the agonizing fear that she'd just traded a lifetime of love for the opportunity to get herself killed.

MEGHAN POURED HERSELF a cup of hot tea the next morning and glanced back at the kitchen table where Durk was engrossed in faxes. "Would you like a refill on your coffee?"

"Yeah, thanks," he said without looking up. "Now that everyone has left for church, we can get back down to business."

But he'd been all about business even before they'd left. The verbal clash last night had thrown a suffocating damper on their relationship. Now it seemed that all he wanted was to get his time with her over and done with.

She set his coffee in front of him and slid into the chair next to his, irritated that he'd seemingly been able to push the kiss from his mind while it dominated her thoughs. It had set her on fire. Had her job really meant so much to her that she'd walked away from Durk rather than cut back on the danger? What kind of danger junkie was she?

Durk pushed one of the fax printouts of her phone activity in her direction.

"The names that have a line through them are the ones that Jackson Phelps feels don't deserve further scrutiny at this time."

She looked at the first name that had been marked out. It was a pharmacy. The corresponding address was near her condo. She agreed that it was likely irrelevant.

"What about the names with asterisks by them?"

"Those are the phone numbers that Jackson considers to be possibly relevant. As you'll notice some of the phone numbers couldn't be cross-referenced with names or addresses."

She scanned the list.

Roderick Farmington.

Dwight Richmond.

Evan Byers.

Jack Little.

And the list went on. The frustrations were piling on like building blocks, and the tower was about ready to tumble and take her down with it. She could be staring at the name of Roxanne and Ben's killer and still be clueless.

The headache returned, and she was starting to wonder if it might be more stress related than a side effect of the injury. She let the sheet of paper slip through her fingers and fall to the table. "Nothing looks familiar."

"Maybe we should drop it for a while. It's obvious that memory retrieval can't be forced."

"Agreed. I think I'll try out the swing on the front porch. I need some fresh air."

"Are you dizzy?"

"No, Durk. And if you're thinking of keeping the nurse on duty for my sake, it really is a waste of money."

"The nurse basically told Mother and me the same thing. But she's here for another day for Aunt Sybil, so if you change your mind, page her."

"I will."

The phone rang as Meghan made her exit. She hesitated to see if it was Lucy on the line.

Durk followed the hello with a quick "She's here. Can I ask what this is about?"

His expression darkened as he handed her his phone. "It's Detective Smart."

She didn't need the detective's harassment right now. She skipped the small talk. "If you're calling to see if I've remembered anything that can help you, the answer is no."

"Actually I'm calling to tell you that some workmen found your car at daybreak."

"Where?"

"It was submerged in a creek that runs behind an old warehouse just south of I-20."

Her blood ran cold. If things had gone the killer's way, her body would have been in that car.

"We had it pulled from the water a few minutes ago," Smart continued.

"Have you seen the car?"

"I'm standing next to it right now. We found a suitcase in the trunk that I'm assuming is not yours."

"I wouldn't know."

"It's full of what appears to be human bones."

She reeled at the news. "Where do you go from here?"

"That's what I want to talk to you about."

WITHIN THIRTY MINUTES Meghan was in the passenger seat of Durk's car and they were heading toward her office for her first trip back there since Ben's body had been found.

Their meeting with Detective Smart was at his request. Holding the meeting in her office was her idea.

Since Durk was the first to see the crime scene, she wanted to see it through his eyes. Once she'd moved back to her condo, there might not be another chance to have him walk her through what she'd found.

In fact she might not ever be face-to-face with him again.

The detective was waiting inside her office

when they arrived. He had little new information that he could—or would—share.

The bones in the trunk had been delivered to forensics for further examination. Meghan's car had been towed to the evidence lot. Neither Ben's computer nor hers was in the car.

Bottom line—they were no closer to indentifying the killer than they were before recovering the vehicle.

The only positive was that Smart had stopped treating Durk like a suspect. She figured the chief of police had gotten wind of that and put an immediate quietus on it. When a detective accused a man of Durk Lambert's status of a crime, he'd best have convincing evidence to back it up.

"We have a homicide and a suitcase full of bones," Smart said. "Now all we need is a viable suspect."

"Any real clues as to his identity yet?" Durk asked. "Like fingerprints or motive?"

"No comment."

Smart turned to Meghan and pulled a grainy computer picture from his pocket of a stout young man with shaggy hair that hung to his shoulders. "Do you recognize this man?"

"No. Should I?"

"Does the name Edward Byers mean anything to you?"

"Edward? No. But I apparently made a phone call to an *Evan* Byers last month."

Smart's brows arched and he gave her that gotcha look.

"Hate to bust your bubble, Detective, but I'm not holding out on you. I don't remember the call. I got the name from the cell phone company, probably the same way you came up with it. Are Evan and Edward related?"

"They're brothers—identical twins. You'd never know it. Evan is clean-cut, muscular, nice-looking. At least he is in his Facebook photos."

"What do you have on the Byers brothers?"

"Not much on Evan. Clean record except for some unpaid parking tickets."

"How old are they?" Meghan asked.

"Twenty-nine. Evan's been divorced for over three years. No kids."

"What does he do for a living?" Durk asked.

"Nothing at the present. He's one of those brainiacs, was working as a biochemist for a pharmaceutical company until three months ago when the government stopped funding the grant for his cancer research project."

Meghan made a few notes on a pad she'd

picked up from what had evidently been Ben's desk. "What's the scoop on Edward?"

"Not so squeaky-clean. He's been arrested on numerous charges dating back to high school, ranging from shoplifting to writing hot checks on his brother's bank account. The most recent arrest was last year. He did six months' jail time for stalking a UT coed. He's out on parole now."

Meghan put down her notepad. "Have you questioned him?"

"No, but I will once I find and arrest him for violating the conditions of his parole. I've got an APB out on him."

"Have you talked to Evan?"

"I'm on my way to his house when I leave here. Hopefully he'll cooperate without my having to bring him in for official questioning."

"I'd appreciate it if you'd keep me informed as to what you find out," Meghan said.

"And I'm ordering you to do the same for me. If I find out you know the identity of Ben's killer and don't tell me I swear I'll see that you lose your P.I. license."

She stretched her neck without breaking eye contact. "I wouldn't blame you, Detective—were I to do that."

"And don't try to contact either Evan or Edward Byers on your own, Meghan. That's also an order."

"Is that all?"

"For now, except that you can officially have your office back. The CSU has what they need. If I decide I need access to your files, I'll get a search warrant."

"I'm sure you would."

Smart scanned the office area again, slowly, as if he expected some vital clue he'd missed earlier would jump out at him. When he turned back to Meghan his demeanor seemed far less provoking. "I'm sorry about Ben," he admitted. "It's tough losing a partner. It'll make you want to do everything you can to get the man who killed him. But don't. Just give me the name and let me take care of it."

"Thanks, Detective."

"I hear the funeral's on Tuesday," Smart said. "I guess you'll be there."

"Most likely." Though she wasn't sure yet how she'd face his wife when she couldn't even remember Ben.

She waited until Smart had left before she walked around the desk and sat down in Ben's chair.

She picked up the framed picture of him

and a striking young woman she assumed was Mary Nell.

Speak to me, Ben. Tell me who killed you. Help me find him. And if my mistakes or misjudgments caused your death, forgive me. Please forgive me.

If his death were her fault, she would never forgive herself.

"Tell me what you saw when you walked through the door, Durk. Walk me through what happened and try to leave nothing out."

Durk covered it all. The gore. The chaos. The cops pointing their guns at him.

He went through everything step by step. Nothing he said took her closer to finding the killer.

In spite of the tension between her and Durk, she couldn't wait to go back to the ranch.

CAROLINA SAT ON the top step, her full skirt pulled around her so that it fell to her ankles. Belle was in her lap, playing with a set of plastic keys and laughing at Tommy, who was tumbling in the grass.

Her neighbor from a few ranches away sat next to her. R. J. Dalton was an argumentative old coot who managed to make enemies of almost everyone who knew him with his outspoken opinions on politics, religion and life in general.

Sometimes he got on Carolina's nerves, too, but today he was in a rare sociable mood and actually carrying on a decent conversation. Or perhaps it was just that she needed the diversion.

Not only was she concerned about Durk, but Damien had been so quiet and distracted at lunch that she knew he must be worried about Durk, as well.

"I'm thinking of selling my land," R.J. said.

"Do you need the money?"

"Nope. But I'm not gonna live forever. No use holding on to it."

"You're not sick, are you?"

"I'm too ornery to get sick. You know that. I'm just thinking of selling, that's all. If you or your sons are interested, give me a call. Make an honest offer, I'll think on it."

"Don't you have children, R.J.?"

"You don't see any of them hanging around pouring honey on my biscuits, do you?"

"That goes two ways. When's the last time you called them?"

"You can say it plain, Carolina. I was a lousy father. I can't undo what's done. Besides, that's got nothing to do with selling my land."

"I know you don't need the money, and you

can't take it with you. Call your sons. Offer the ranch to them."

"Why do you think I want to sell it? I don't want them showing up after I'm dead like vultures looking to pick my bones clean. They'd probably end up bulldozing beautiful farmland and ranch land to build a subdivision with look-alike houses and a golf course running through my favorite fishing hole."

"How many children do you have?"

"By which wife?"

"All of them."

"Five sons. And a daughter who's likely as much a hellcat as her mother is."

"Write them all a letter and invite them out to see you," Carolina said. "Get to know them. Give them a chance to get to know you."

"Nah. It's too late for that. This dog is all done huntin'. If you're interested in the land, give me a holler. Otherwise I'll find another buyer."

He stood to go back to his old beat-up pickup truck. If someone didn't know better, they'd think he was financially destitute. Carolina knew better.

She couldn't resist leaving him with a final thought. "You might find out that your children are the very best of you, R.J."

"But I might find out they're the worst."

Durk and Meghan pulled up just as R.J. was driving away. A black sedan Carolina didn't recognize followed them into the driveway. It parked behind them, and two men she'd never seen before stepped out. Carolina had no idea why they were there, but she was almost certain the reason wouldn't be to her liking.

"Come here, Tommy," Carolina said firmly. "Let's go find your daddy."

"Don't wanna go inside."

She hurried down the steps and grabbed his hand, but Durk and the two men were already facing each other on the walk.

"Are you looking for someone?" Durk asked.

"I'm looking for my daughter. She's approximately nine months old. Her name is Belle."

Carolina's chest constricted, squeezing her heart until it felt like it would crack from the pressure. Tommy yanked free of her hand and ran to Durk. She tightened her arms around Belle.

"What's your name?" Durk asked.

"His name is Juan Perez," the other man answered for him. "I'm his attorney, Felipe Torres. We were told the baby's foster parents are here and we'd like to talk to them."

Carolina had to force herself to breathe as Durk invited the two men inside. She'd always known there was a chance Belle's biological father would come for her. She'd tried to prepare herself for this moment ever since sweet Belle had come into their lives.

But she wasn't ready. She'd never be ready, no more than she could be ready to give up her heart.

Chapter Sixteen

When Meghan woke up Tuesday morning and realized that the amnesia still held her memories hostage, she knew it was time to leave the Bent Pine Ranch and go back to her condo in the city.

She was a stranger whom Durk had insinuated into his family's lives at the worst possible time. They were in a state of anxiety as they waited on the results of the paternity test to determine whether this Juan Perez was indeed baby Belle's biological father. The easy warmth and teasing were gone. They did not need Meghan and her problems added to their own.

She'd made the decision and laid the groundwork so that there would be no reason for Durk to protest—not that she was convinced that he'd want to. She'd called the complex manager yesterday and had them send in a cleaning crew to ready her condo.

She'd made arrangements for a car to pick her

up on Thursday for her appointment to see Dr. Levy and to get her sutures removed. And she was packed and ready to go home.

She had only one request of Durk and that was that he stop by the funeral home so that she could pay her last respects to a friend and co-worker she couldn't remember.

Dressed and ready to go, she went searching for Durk and found him in the kitchen having coffee with Carolina. She told both of them her plans at the same time.

Durk didn't protest until Carolina had said her goodbyes and left the room. "Nothing like waiting until the last minute to spring this on me, Meghan."

"Your family doesn't need a guest to entertain at a time like this."

"If you think I'm leaving you at the condo alone with the killer still on the loose, you'd best think again. It's not going to happen."

"I can't stay here."

"Then we'll stay somewhere else, or I'll stay with you at the condo. You choose, but I'm not leaving you alone."

"Why are you doing this, Durk? You make it impossible for me to leave and impossible to stay. We're constantly torn. The attraction is maddening, but the things that push us apart are even stronger. There's no way to win."

"And no way I can lose you to a madman. Give this a few more days, Meghan. Give the amnesia time to run its course so that you know who you were when it all backfired and fell apart."

"And if I don't?"

"Then I camp outside your door."

She knew he meant it. That was Durk. It was the cowboy creed. He wanted her safe. He just didn't want her.

But there was a limit to how much rejection her heart could take. "I'll give it two more days," she said. "After that, you have to let go and I have to find a way to keep myself safe. I'll buy another gun, put triple locks on all the doors or hire a bodyguard if it comes to that."

"Do you still want to go to the funeral home?"

Actually, she didn't. It wouldn't give her closure. It wouldn't bring Ben back to life. It wouldn't stop the killer from killing again.

"I have a better idea," she said, the plan already forming in her mind. "Let's pay a visit to Evan Byers."

"Detective Smart ordered you to stay away from him."

"I'm not under arrest. Neither is Evan Byers.

He's not even a suspect. He's just someone whose phone number showed up on my phone. My talking to him is not breaking any law."

"That doesn't make it wise."

"If you don't want to go, just say so, Durk. I can get a car and driver."

He stared at her as if he'd like to wring her neck—or kiss her. With Durk it wasn't always easy to distinguish between the two.

"I'll meet you at the car in ten minutes," he said. "But remember that I'm doing this under protest."

EVAN'S HOME WAS in an eclectic neighborhood of houses built in the 1930s to 1940s and newly constructed townhomes. His was of the former category, a neat raised cottage with painted shutters on the windows and pots of greenery hanging from the porch banisters.

He answered the door in a pair of cutoff jeans and no shirt or shoes even though the temperature was only in the high fifties. He stared critically at Meghan. "What happened to you?"

"I was in a car wreck," she lied.

"I'm sorry." He looked confused. "How can I help you?"

"My name is Meghan Sinclair and this is my partner, Durk. We're here to see Edward."

"He's not around right now. I'm Evan, his brother. What do you want to see him about? Perhaps I can help."

"Someone called me from the phone number. I think it might have been Edward."

"Perhaps. It wasn't me."

"Do you know how I can get in touch with him? I heard he was in some trouble with the law and I thought I might be able to help him," Meghan said.

"Are you certain you're not from the Dallas Police Department?"

"Positive. I'm a private detective."

"As far as I know Edward doesn't need anything or anyone investigated."

"Really? Because a friend of mine told my partner and me that Edward was eager to talk to someone about helping him get out of trouble with the law."

"They're mistaken. Edward's not in any trouble."

Either Evan was lying or he was in denial.

"Then you don't know how I can get in touch with Edward?"

"Not at the moment."

"What about later today?"

"Why don't you give me your number? I can have him call you."

"There's not really any reason for him to call me if he's not in any trouble," Meghan said, baiting him.

"He didn't do anything," Evan insisted. "He's assured me that he is walking the line, but he says once the cops pin one thing on you, they try to pin everything on you. There's a Detective Smart who I believe has it in for my brother."

Evan was clearly the enabler. He'd probably been making excuses for his twin brother all his life. A stalker. A pervert. A serial killer. *Get real, Evan.*

She'd love to snoop around the house and basement and see if there were any more suitcases full of bones lying around.

She was about to ask to use his bathroom just for a chance to snoop more when a couple of dogs started howling and yelping as if they were in a major fight. Evan excused himself to go and see what was wrong with his dog. Durk followed him.

Meghan went straight to the basement.

She opened the door and flicked on the light. Nothing happened. The bulb had most likely burned out. But there was enough light from the hall that she could see the pictures pasted on the walls.

A mix of paintings and photographs of men

having sex with women dressed in similar clothes to what Connie had described. Vulgar, disgusting, pornographic images that made Meghan's skin crawl.

Meghan held on to the railing and took the rickety steps all the way down. There was just enough light from the open doorway to let her see shapes and outlines.

It surprised her how neat the area was. She took a few steps away from the stairs and that's when she saw it. Her heart jumped to her throat. She didn't even try to hold back the scream.

Chapter Seventeen

Durk heard the scream and took off running, racing through the house and calling Meghan's name. If he'd let something happen to her... No, he couldn't think that way.

"Meghan!" He called her name again.

"Down here. In the basement. Call Detective Smart. Call him now."

He took the dark steps two at a time. He saw the body before he saw her. The man was dangling by his neck from a gnarled rope that hung from an old meat hook in the ceiling.

Meghan was slumped against the wall, a little green, but not hurt. He scooped her into his arms just as Evan reached the bottom of the stairs.

He let out a bloodcurdling scream and then wrapped himself around the legs of the dead man.

"They killed him," he cried. "They killed my brother. They never gave him a chance."

"It looks as if he hanged himself," Durk said as he dialed 911.

"Because they wouldn't leave him alone," Evan wailed. "They were never going to leave him alone."

Sobs racked Evan's body.

Durk didn't know if Edward Byers was guilty of murder. That would be for a judge and jury to decide, but he knew that at least three people were dead. Roxanne Latimer. Ben Conroe. And now Edward Byers.

For the first time he understood a little better why Meghan threw herself into these cases with such reckless abandon.

Justice should be served.

They were all three still in the basement with the body when sirens screamed and cops rushed the house.

There were a lot of unanswered questions, but Smart could take charge from here on out. He was taking Meghan home.

MEMORIES FLOODED Meghan's mind as she walked out of Evan's house and into the blinding afternoon sunshine. Shock and grief convened in frenzied waves as the events of the investigation leading up to her attack stormed her mind.

Durk pulled her in his arms to steady her.

"It's all coming back to me," she murmured. "Everything." Tears filled her eyes and ran down her cheeks. "We had him. Ben was the one who put the final pieces together. We knew it was Edward. We were so close."

"It's okay," he soothed. "It's all over. You got your man."

"But I lost Ben. The world lost Ben. Mary Nell lost her husband and the father of her child. Oh, God, if we could only go back. If things had gone the way we planned."

Durk helped her into the car, then put his arm around her shoulder and held her while she cried.

"How were things supposed to go down the night you were attacked?"

"Nothing should have happened that night. I met with Edward that afternoon. I knew he was the one who'd killed Roxanne and others, as well. But I needed more evidence."

"So you were going to let him abduct you and take you prisoner?"

"No. Nothing like that. I had it all planned. The date, the time, the place. I would go to the police and talk them into putting a wire on me. When he made his move they could be there in seconds."

"But Edward figured it out?"

"He was shrewd. Always cunning. He never

made a mistake. That's how he got away with so many murders for so long."

"Yet he went to jail for stalking a coed?"

"I can't imagine what happened there. But he didn't slip up with Roxanne."

"How did he take her from the pub without anyone hearing her cry for help?"

"She never cried for help. She was meeting her lover. They'd met in a chat room on line and then exchanged private email addresses. They were finally going to meet in person that night. The text was her signal to dump her friends."

"How did you learn that?"

"Through the computer of one of her friends. Roxanne had used it a few nights when hers needed repairs. Fortunately, the computer had gone on the blink at just the right time to record her last messages."

"But not in time to save her. So sad," Durk said. "A young life wasted to satisfy a depraved pervert."

"And Edward killed over and over and over again. Someone had to stop him. But why did we have to lose Ben?"

"Somehow Edward figured out that you were not what you seemed. The only way to stop you from having him arrested was to kill both you and Ben."

"We won't know the full truth until the investigation is complete, but at least we know that Edward Byers won't go on killing innocent women to satisfy his need for cheap thrills."

"Let's get out of here," Durk said. "This time when we get to the ranch you really can relax."

"I'm not going back to the ranch, Durk. The threat of danger is over. If I went back now, it would be about us. And there is no us."

"If that's the way you want it."

"I'm not the one who made the rules."

MEGHAN SAID GOODBYE to Durk, probably for the last time, and then walked to her bedroom and fell across the bed. They'd made a stop at her office on the way back to her condo. It had seemed the fitting place to say her goodbye to Ben.

Tomorrow she'd go see Mary Nell, but she just couldn't handle it today.

She'd lost Durk forever, too. She closed her eyes, sure exhaustion would take hold. Instead a new surge of memories took hold.

Meghan stepped out of the elevator and headed to her condo. A lot of preparation remained to be done before tomorrow evening, but her main priority now was kicking out of the 4.8-inch stilettos and shedding the sickening blond wig. Those along with the schoolgirl dress and the Christmas-red lipstick made her look like a cross between Little Bo Peep and Lady Gaga.

Just the way lover boy liked his dates to look—perverted, demented soul that he was. He'd gone to such lengths to set his brother up for his crimes. He thought he was too smart to get caught. He had a plan for every eventuality. He had no conscience, no guilt, no shame.

That's why he'd show up tomorrow night, never suspecting that she'd be wired. This time when he went in for the abduction, the police would be waiting. This time she'd play by their rules.

But she had to work fast. She had a date with a killer. Evan Byers was about to meet his match.

Meghan jumped from the bed as the truth rolled in her mind.

They'd gotten it all wrong. Edward wasn't their killer and he wasn't the one who'd attacked her. Evan was the guilty one. He'd plotted, he'd schemed and he'd carried out his plans. The only thing that had kept him from abducting and raping and torturing her had been Bill Mackey.

And once she was in his possession, he'd have gone back to put the bullet in Ben's head, using her gun. It had all been a sick joke to him, a mockery of everything decent in the world.

Something moved behind her. Meghan jumped from the bed as someone grabbed her from behind.

"Did anyone ever tell you that there's such a thing as being too smart, Meghan Sinclair?"

The question was rhetorical. He was on top of her with one hand over her mouth and the other ripping away her blouse.

"Time to get dressed for your lover, Meghan. And it won't be Durk."

Meghan struggled to get away. She could not die at the hands of this madman. She refused to be just another victim. She couldn't bear to be a participant in one of his depraved fantasies.

But the fight was futile. Even healthy, she'd have been no match for his strength. She finally quit fighting it and let her mind float back to how it had felt in Durk's arms the first time they'd made love.

They'd been magic from the very first kiss. She'd thrown the magic away. Now she would never get it back.

She'd never get the chance to tell Durk that she loved him more than life itself.

Chapter Eighteen

Durk pulled into traffic and let the facts surrounding Edward's suicide try to fall into some kind of cohesive pattern. They refused.

It didn't add up. It would have made more sense if brainiac Evan was their serial killer. He had the gray matter between his ears. He had the look to pull it off. He had the basement where he could have tortured his victims—and created a fake suicide. He had the opportunity to hang the revolting pictures—all part of a detailed plan to convince the police of Edward's guilt.

Edward had...nothing.

Could the real killer have possibly fooled them all? Durk took out his phone and called Meghan's condo. Her phone rang six times before the answering machine picked up.

Adrenaline rushed through him as panic set in. Evan could have fooled them—but only if Meghan's memory had not fully kicked in. Edward and Evan looked nothing alike. She'd had a coffee date with the killer. Even though her attacker had been masked, she could have easily told the Byers twins apart just by their builds.

Durk swerved into a U-turn, leaving a line of cars blowing their horns and shouting curses as he sped back to Meghan's condo. He grabbed his pistol from beneath the seat and took the stairs to the fifth floor, running so fast his feet barely skimmed the wood.

He knocked once and then burst into the condo. Muffled sounds sent him running to the bedroom.

"Drop the gun or I kill her."

Evan held a knife in his right hand, the tip of it pressing into the flesh just below Meghan's jugular vein.

"Let her go, Evan. It's over. I figured it out and I've already called Detective Smart. You're going to prison and have a whole new set of playmates."

It was a bluff. Evan didn't buy it.

"I said drop the gun."

"You can kill her, Evan, but you can't kill us both before I take you out."

"I'm not kidding. Drop the gun."

He wasn't kidding, but he was sweating bullets. But so was Durk, deep inside where it could only be felt. He dropped the gun before Evan panicked and sliced Meghan's throat.

"I'm going out of here with Meghan, just as I'd originally planned. Stand back, Durk Lambert. You're not in control this time."

With the knife still at Meghan's throat, he tugged her to her feet and held her in front of him as he made his way to the door.

"Bitsy, you come back here now!"

The overly friendly dog from across the hall raced through the door Durk had left open. He jumped up, his front paws reaching to the middle of Evan's back. Evan lost his balance, and in that split second Durk took him down.

They wrestled over the knife while Bitsy's owner screamed and Bitsy almost licked a yelping Evan to death. By the time the fight was over and the knife was in Durk's hand, Sara Cunningham's entire extended family had gathered in the hallway to watch the show.

"Someone call 911," Durk said as he kept Evan pinned to the floor.

It wasn't until after the cops had left with Evan in cuffs that Durk finally got to pull Meghan into his arms. Adrenaline was still pumping through his veins. His heart was pounding. His emotions were in overdrive. But there was one thing he was certain of. "I have never been so scared. I don't want to ever let you go. I love you, Meghan. Boy, do I love you."

"I love you, too, Durk. I did from the very first kiss. I remember it all now. I was wrong, so very wrong. I love what I do, but you are the most important thing in my life."

"We'll work it out, Meghan. Somehow we'll work it out. And we'll get a very large dog."

Epilogue

Strings of pearly blue Christmas lights sparkled in the low branches of the oak trees that Hugh's grandfather had planted years ago to shade the house from the afternoon sun. Christmas carols wafted through the air accompanied by the sounds of laughter and tinkling glasses as the first of the guests began to trickle in at the Bent Pine Ranch.

But for now it was mostly family. Carolina liked it like that, though it made her miss Hugh even more. He'd have loved being here tonight, seeing his three sons so very much in love and the family growing.

And as cautious as Carolina had been about Meghan in the beginning, she had to admit she loved having her around. She kept things exciting. Best of all she made Durk happier than she'd ever seen him.

Tommy came up and grabbed Carolina's hand. "Wanna dance, Gramma?"

"I do if you'll be my partner."

"Be your partner."

She went with him to the dance floor and let him dance around her while she swayed to the music.

It was going to be a wonderful night.

THE DANCE FLOOR was packed. Meghan liked it that way. It meant she got to snuggle all the closer to Durk.

"You've outdone yourself tonight. You look stunning."

"With my shaved head?"

"It's starting to grow out. Besides, it reminds me how lucky I am that you're alive. And you do look fantastic. That red dress looks dynamite on you. Your gorgeous legs look a mile long in those gold stilettos. And you can still walk. Amazing."

"I can do more than walk in them."

He nuzzled her ear. "I can't wait for you to show me, but maybe you should save that until we're alone."

"I just might show you a thing or two tonight. When is your mother going to make the promised surprise announcement?"

"Soon, I'm sure."

"Then we should move over to the edge of the dance floor. She wants the family all together for this."

Meghan could barely hide her excitement. She loved Durk so much she was constantly giddy with excitement. He seemed to love her just as much, but there had been no mention of marriage.

Was that what he'd meant by "we'll work it out"? That they'd be lovers and nothing more? At one point in her life that would have been more than enough. She'd always been so independent.

But she hadn't been in love then. Now she wanted it all. The ring and the commitment. And a few years down the road—when she was ready to slow down and perhaps teach private investigating instead of living it—she wanted a family. Two kids at least, maybe three. Definitely a boy who looked like Durk.

But first, a husband. And she had a sneaking suspicion that the surprise announcement was supposed to be an engagement. Only Durk still hadn't asked her to marry him and time was running out.

A few minutes later, the band quit playing and Carolina stepped to the microphone.

"I want to welcome all of you to share this blessed holiday season with us. But this week our family received an extraspecial holiday blessing. It's especially fitting this time of the year when we celebrate the birth of a baby, God's son, for us to share our news with you. Only I'm going to let Damien and Emma do the honors."

Damien wrapped his arm around his wife's shoulder. "Belle's father finally made his decision. His new wife is pregnant and they're moving back to her home country of Guatemala. He's asked Emma and me if we will adopt Belle legally. We've said yes."

There was not a dry eye at the party when he handed the mike back to Carolina.

"So Merry Christmas to all of you," Carolina said. "Now, let's party."

"One more announcement," Durk said as he walked to the bandstand. "I'd like to announce my engagement to a woman who brought the magic into my life. But first I guess I should ask her to marry me. Meghan, would you come up here, please?"

Her face turned as red as her dress as she joined him, but joy filled her soul.

He dropped to one knee. "Will you marry me, Meghan Sinclair, and let me spend the rest of my life loving you?"

"Yes."

The chant of "louder" went up from every corner of the grounds.

"Yes. Yes, I will. And there will be no more blurring of the lines," she whispered. "I have no plans to make you the most eligible widower in Dallas."

He kissed her and pulled her into his arms as the band started playing a country love song.

"The P.I. and CEO, together again," he whispered. "And this time, it's forever."

* * * * *